W9-BYB-158

THE EARL OF KENT

A League of Rogues Novel and a Wicked Earls' Club Novel

LAUREN SMITH

This book is a work of fiction. Names, characters, places, and incidents are the product of the author's imagination or are used fictitiously. Any resemblance to actual events, locales, or persons, living or dead, is coincidental.

Copyright © 2019 by Lauren Smith

Excerpt from The Earl of Kiross by Meara Platt (c) By Meara Platt

Cover Art by Jaycee DeLorenzo

The League of Rogues (R) is a federally registered trademark owned by Lauren Smith and cannot be copied or used without the expression permission of Lauren Smith.

All rights reserved. In accordance with the U.S. Copyright Act of 1976, the scanning, uploading, and electronic sharing of any part of this book without the permission of the publisher constitutes unlawful piracy and theft of the author's intellectual property. If you would like to use material from the book (other than for review purposes), prior written permission must be obtained by contacting the publisher at lauren@laurensmithbooks.com. Thank you for your support of the author's rights.

The publisher is not responsible for websites (or their content) that are not owned by the publisher.

ISBN: 978-1-947206-79-3 (e-book edition)

ISBN: 978-1-947206-80-9 (print edition)

PROLOGUE

*L**ondon, December 1816*
     Fifteen-year-old Ella Humphrey was caught in a dream as she leaned over the wooden banister overlooking the entryway to her home. Two young men had come in through the door, shaking snow off their Hessian boots and removing their hats as they talked jovially. One was her older brother Graham, and the other...the other was a man she'd never seen before. Tall, dark haired, with a deep rich laugh that sent butterflies fluttering inside her stomach.

"It's rather tragic, don't you think?"

Ella jolted and turned to find her mother, Violet, the Dowager Countess of Lonsdale, behind her. She looked sad as she too looked down at the pair of young men.

"What's tragic?" asked Ella.

"Graham's friend, Lord Kent. His parents both died of typhus a month ago I heard, while visiting relatives in

Scotland. He's only twenty-three, far too young to be an orphan." Violet stroked Ella's blonde hair as Ella gazed down at the handsome man in the entrance hall below.

Kent was tall, like her two brothers, Charles and Graham, but where they had hair like burnished gold, this man's was dark. As he turned their way, she caught a glimpse of his blue eyes. He threw back his head and laughed at something Graham had said, but his laughter didn't reach those sorrowful eyes. She saw only pain, a pain she could tell he was trying to bury.

"Why don't you go to the library and find a book to read this evening? I must see that Kent is settled for the night."

Ella blushed. "He's to stay here? With us?"

Violet nodded. "Why of course he is. Graham said he doesn't wish to stay in his family home in the country. It must be painful to see reminders of his parents. He is to stay with us through Christmas."

Ella remained still as her mother walked downstairs and introduced herself to Kent. Ella fisted her hands in her skirts as an odd, almost wild longing made her chest ache whenever she looked at Lord Kent.

"What are you up to, little bit?" her eldest brother, Charles, the current Earl of Lonsdale, teased her as he came up from behind. She pointed down at Kent without a word.

"Ah... Nice fellow, Kent. Shame about his parents."

She blushed again and looked at Charles. He was so much older than her, by eleven years, that it often felt a lifetime spanned between them. Their father had died when she was young, and Ella had been raised by Charles and her mother. Her eldest brother was a surrogate father to her in many ways.

"Why the blush, little bit?" he asked, his gray eyes twinkling. "Fancy him, do you?"

Ella bit her lip, too shy to admit that Kent was fast claiming her full focus.

"Well, he's not for you, love. You're far too young and too sweet to marry. And any man who wants you will have to answer to me first." Charles chuckled as though his comment was amusing, but she saw nothing funny about it. Having an overprotective pair of brothers was going to be a problem once she came out in society and began her hunt for a husband.

Ella shrugged off Charles's hand when he tried to ruffle her curls. She wasn't a little girl anymore, and she didn't like it when he ruined her carefully designed hairstyles.

"Never grow up," Charles said in a suddenly solemn tone. "I think it would break my heart." He walked back down the hallway to his chambers, leaving her alone once again. When she sought out Lord Kent down in the hall below, he was gone. Kent, Graham, and her mother had all vanished from view.

With a sigh of disappointment, Ella wandered down into the library, where she retrieved a book on the history of Pompeii. The doomed city consumed by fire and ash always caught her attention when she needed a distraction. But she did not stay in the library to read; she instead went to the billiard room and curled up in a large leather armchair facing the fireplace.

The warmth of the fire kept the winter chill outside at bay. Charles had said that this chair had been their father's favorite. She wished she could remember him more clearly. All she could see of Guy Humphrey was a smiling man with blond hair and gray eyes who gazed down upon her from an oil portrait in the main gallery of their home, a man who looked much like Charles, but her memories of him were hazy. Sitting here in this chair, she felt connected to him, and yet she knew how silly that sounded. When she was younger, she'd often imagined he was sitting there with her in the chair, holding her with invisible arms. She'd outgrown such imaginative thoughts now, but she couldn't resist claiming the chair each night as she read.

She opened her book, turning to the first page, even though she had read this book twice already. A quarter of an hour later, as she nearly finished the first chapter, the door to the billiard room opened and someone entered. Ella peeped around the back of the chair to see who it was and froze when she realized it was Lord Kent. He was alone and didn't know she was there. He walked over to the billiard table and placed his hands on the gleaming walnut frame of the table. Then his head dropped forward between his shoulders, and he let out a deep sigh. It was clear he had come here to be alone.

Ella closed her book and tucked it into the seat as

she held her breath. She couldn't escape the room without him noticing, and she could not remain here either lest she disturb his solitude. Finally, she summoned her courage and coughed politely.

Kent turned to face her, his blue eyes widening as he spotted her in the chair.

"Oh...I beg your pardon. I thought I was alone." His face turned ruddy as he looked away. For a second Ella thought he'd been about to cry. Men didn't cry. At least, she'd never seen her brothers cry. No, that wasn't true. She remembered, hazily, Graham crying after their father died. That must be why Kent was upset. He had lost his parents recently.

"I'm sorry. I didn't mean to disturb you," she said, her heart racing as she left her chair and started toward the door.

"Wait. No, don't go. Perhaps I do need someone to be here with me." He chuckled dryly, and the sound tugged at her heart. She had the strangest urge to throw her arms about his chest and hug him. Yet she didn't dare, as that would be highly improper.

"We could play billiards," she suggested. Games often distracted her when she was feeling unhappy.

"That is an excellent idea." He smiled broadly as he stacked the ivory balls on the table. Ella retrieved two billiard cues and handed him one.

"You must be..." He tapped his chin, pretending to think before he spoke. "Ella, yes? Graham and Charles's younger sister?"

She nodded eagerly. "I'm fifteen," she told him, then blushed, feeling silly about saying it so proudly. Only a child went around spouting her age.

"That's a fine age. You're almost grown. In three years, you'll be debuting for your first season." Kent's charming smile sent another flock of butterflies to her belly. Why did this man have such an effect on her? She'd met plenty of Graham's friends before tonight, and yet she'd never felt like this.

"You're Graham's age, aren't you? Twenty-three?" she asked.

"I am. Positively ancient, eh?" He waggled his eyebrows, and Ella laughed, even though it made her breathless. She coughed suddenly as she tried to catch her breath.

Kent reached out to her. "Are you all right? Your face is quite red."

"Yes." She panted a little. "I was born early. Mama says that I'm delicate. I'm not, though," she insisted. She hated being called *fragile* or *delicate*. Everyone treated her like a newborn babe. But she wasn't weak or helpless.

"Well, it sounds like you get breathless when you're a bit excited. We must therefore endeavor to bore you to tears." Kent was teasing her again. With a wave, he gestured to the billiard table. "Why don't you take the first hit?"

She regained her breath and watched him set one red ball and two white balls on the table. One white ball had a black spot on it to distinguish it from the other white ball. She took careful aim at the red target. She struck the red ball, which in turn struck the other white ball, and all three balls rolled around on the green baize cover of the table wildly.

Kent whistled in appreciation as the red target ball came close to sinking into a leather pocket on the side of the table.

"Shall we play life pool?" Kent ventured, leaning his hip on the billiard table. Ella couldn't help but admire his tall form, his lean legs outlined in buff-colored trousers, and the way his burgundy waistcoat molded to his chest. Another surge of fluttering in her stomach excited her all over again. She smoothed her hands down the pale-pink muslin of her gown and hoped she looked as pretty as the ladies he must be used to spending his time with. She had on a high-necked gown, suitable for a young woman not yet out in society, and her hair was down except for a part pulled away from her face and tied back with a dark-pink bow. Ella tried not to think how girlish she must appear to him.

"How does one play life pool?" she asked, trying to mirror his relaxed posture. It was a bit more difficult to do in a gown, and her hip slipped off the table's lip the first time she tried.

"We each have three lives. You lose a life when the other person sinks your target ball into the pocket." He went over to the rack and plucked a second ball, this one bright green, and set it down. "This will be my target ball. Yours shall be the red."

"And after three lives?" she asked.

"You can purchase more lives and continue to play. That's called starring. But you can only star once per game."

"I think I understand." She held out her hand. "Shall we shake upon it, Lord Kent?"

Lord Kent's eyes glinted with mirth. "Call me Phillip, please." He placed his hand in hers and gave it a hearty shake. She felt a little dizzy at the power of it and the warmth between their palms. His dark hair, cut a little too long, fell into his eyes as he towered over her.

She was suddenly a little afraid and incredibly excited to be playing a game of billiards alone with him. This must be how grown-up ladies felt. She had spied on Charles and Graham often enough as they had lured women away from balls thrown at the Lonsdale family estate. She knew that men and women often kissed and embraced when alone together. Being caught alone with a man could ruin a lady, she knew that as well, but Phillip was a handsome one, one of her brother's friends. She could trust him. She was finally going to be a woman and no longer a child.

"Your turn, Phillip," she declared imperiously. He chuckled in reply, then lined up a shot and struck her red ball, sinking it easily into the pocket. It was only then that she realized he had cheated.

"Wait a moment! I hit first before we decided upon the three lives game. My ball was already there. That was too easy for you." She arched a brow, daring him to disagree.

Phillip shot her a teasing smile and then reached over and gave a playful tug on one of her carefully coiffed golden curls.

"All right, you caught me. Consider that point removed. Better?" His lips twisted as he fought off a smile.

"Yes. Now it is my turn." She took aim at his green ball and crowed as she sank it into a corner pocket.

"I think Graham must've taught you how to play this game," Kent muttered as he walked a circle around the table and viewed the advantages of her target ball's position. Then he took aim at her red ball and sank it.

The next few shots kept them equally losing lives, but Kent lost first.

"Does this mean I win?" she asked, bouncing right beside him. She had never won when she played her brothers. She was convinced they cheated, but she'd never been able to prove it.

"I want to purchase another three lives," Phillip announced. "What do you demand in payment, fair lady?"

"Payment?" She paused in her bouncing to think. She felt deliriously giddy in that moment and couldn't seem to stop when she spoke. "A kiss."

Kent's eyes widened as he leaned on his cue and nearly slid off it. "A kiss?"

"Er—yes." What had she been thinking? She had just demanded a kiss from him. If her brothers ever found out...

Kent set his cue down and came up to her until their bodies were almost touching. She could feel the heat emanating from him. It felt good in the chilly room.

"You're a bit young for kisses," he said quietly.

"I'm *not* young," she insisted, hoping he didn't hear the note of desperation in her tone.

"Very well. One kiss." He cupped her face with one hand, and her body seemed to catch fire as he gazed down at her. She closed her eyes, hardly daring to breathe. Everything seemed to be spinning as she waited for the kiss that would change her life.

But when he kissed her, he pressed his lips to her forehead, not her lips. The soft heat of it sent shivers down her body, and she reached up to grasp his arms, wanting to touch him, to hold him, but he had already stepped away before she could. When she opened her eyes, he was retrieving his cue. All she had was the lingering scent of his body and the slowly fading heat from where he'd been pressed close to her.

"Your turn, I believe," he said politely.

There was a slight hesitation, a distance that he put between them now that made her eyes sting. He hadn't wanted to kiss her—he hadn't even seemed to enjoy it. The womanly confidence she'd felt moments ago had been shattered. A cold knot grew in her stomach, and she could feel the tears coming. But the last thing she wanted was to cry in front of him.

"I'm sorry, I don't wish to play anymore." She dropped her cue and fled the billiard room, not stopping until she reached her bedroom. After slamming the door, she threw herself onto her bed and wept, feeling more and more like the child she realized she still was. A handsome, worldly man like Lord Kent would never see her as a woman. And knowing that broke her heart.

❄

PHILLIP WILKES STARED AT THE OPEN DOORWAY where Ella had fled. He quietly cursed as he bent to retrieve her cue and put away the balls. It seemed he had handled that badly. However, he wasn't sure what the right way to handle that would have been. Coming here for a few days was supposed to relieve him, not cause more stress. He'd had plenty to deal with in the last month since his family solicitor had helped him bury his parents and see to his family's holdings. He still wasn't able to accept that he was now the Earl of Kent. That had been and always would be his father. Yet the title had been thrust upon Phillip.

He'd spent enough time grieving the loss of his parents. He wanted only joy, only happiness right now, yet he'd just made a young lady cry...because he'd had to be honorable. He admitted, at least in his own head, that the little creature was tempting. All that dark-gold hair spilling down her shoulders, and the way her eyes were slightly tilted at the corners gave her an inquisitive, exotic look. She had captured his attention. More than that, she'd made him forget the world for just a short while. But she was a girl, just fifteen. A lifetime separated them, and while he certainly would have loved to steal a kiss, she was far too young.

"Ah, Kent, there you are." Graham stood in the doorway of the billiard room. "I thought perhaps you'd gotten lost and somehow ended up in Soho."

Kent laughed, but there was no mirth in his voice. Coming here with Graham had been enjoyable enough, but every now and then his sorrow was too much, and he needed a moment alone to bury his grief again.

It was why he had fled to this room, but he hadn't expected to run into Graham's little sister. She'd stood there with those big blue-gray eyes, like winter storm clouds. So young, sweet, and innocent.

But he wasn't a villain. He wouldn't kiss her, not in the way her eyes had begged. But perhaps someday, when she was out in society, when she was older. God help him then, because he had a feeling he would be in trouble if he ever had to be alone with her again.

"Are you all right?" Graham asked.

"No," Kent sighed and leaned back against the billiard table. "But there isn't much to be done about it."

"Your parents?" Graham asked.

Phillip nodded. Graham, to his credit, said nothing. He joined Phillip at the billiard table and leaned back against it next to Phillip. A good friend knew when to say nothing and simply offer his company. He was damned lucky to have Graham as a friend. And it was all the more reason why he shouldn't be caught alone with Ella in the future. He doubted Graham would forgive him if he did more than kiss the girl when she was older.

Ella, you will break many a man's heart, but I fear I won't be among them.

Phillip was done with broken hearts, especially his own.

1

ondon, December 1821

L Phillip had always had the devil's own luck, but not tonight. At the moment, he sat at a green baize tabletop playing faro and losing *badly*.

Faro was a game partly of skill and partly of chance, and tonight both were failing him. His opponent, a dark-haired man who'd introduced himself as Daniel Sheffield, was racking up debts against him with an ease that worried Phillip.

"Another hand?" Sheffield challenged. "One good hand would set me right."

Phillip jerked slightly as Graham gripped his arm in warning, but he took no heed.

"Another," Phillip said. He watched the dealer lay out thirteen cards and placed his bet as to which card the dealer would turn up next. Sheffield doubled Phillip's bet, and Graham stiffened beside him.

Phillip tried to keep calm, but the fact was his debts were too high to turn back. But if he won this hand, everything would be fine.

Sheffield's lips twitched a moment before the dealer turned the card over. Phillip's stomach dropped.

"I…" He struggled to breathe. "I may need a few days to collect the finances for you, Mr. Sheffield." His family fortune wasn't enough to cover the sum he'd just wagered and lost.

"I'm afraid I leave in a day's time," Sheffield said. "But perhaps we can come to an arrangement." He leaned in close to whisper to Phillip. "You can pay your debt by fighting in the Lewis Street tunnels in the boxing rings. Mention my name there, and a man with a ledger book will mark your debt as paid. Or I can call it in and take everything, including the clothes off your back."

Phillip found himself nodding numbly as Sheffield left the card room.

"Phillip, what did he say?" Graham asked in an urgent whisper.

Phillip stood, almost swaying on his feet. He felt sick. He reached for his coat and met Graham's frantic gaze. "Not here."

They left the Cockrell pub and stepped out into the icy chill of night. Graham grabbed his arm and jerked him to a halt.

"Phillip, what the devil did he say?"

Phillip's heart felt sluggish. He couldn't meet

Graham's face. "I've no means to pay his debt in a timely fashion. But he offered..."

"What?"

"He has other interests and finds himself in need of someone."

"What do you mean? What interests?"

"Boxing. He feels that I can repay the debt if I agree to fight in the rings on Lewis Street. He has some sort of financial arrangement with those who organize the fights."

Graham's eyes were wide. "Lewis Street?"

"I'm bound there now. Win or lose, he says my debt will be considered paid in full."

"No, Kent, you cannot—"

Phillip spun to face him. "What would you have me do? Better to face a brute in the ring than have every note called in by every financier in London. If word gets out that I have allowed such a debt to be owed, my name will be ruined." He looked away, focusing on the dark streets they stood on, and he tensed at the distant laughter of the men from the pub. "Thank you for trying to stop me from that last hand. I should've listened to you. I'm sorry." Phillip headed toward the nearest intersection and waved for a hackney driver. Graham followed him.

"Well, I won't let you go there alone," Graham said. "Someone's going to have to drag you to a doctor afterward."

Phillip laughed at his friend's attempt to lighten the

mood. "Thank you, but I'd rather prefer to think I stand a chance of winning."

But the truth was, they both knew that the monsters who called themselves men in those Lewis Street rings would try to kill him simply for sport.

The driver stopped at the entrance to Lewis Street, and the two friends climbed out. The darkened alley that led to the tunnels was guarded by a tall, thick-necked brute of a man who grunted when Phillip mentioned Daniel Sheffield's name. He stepped aside and let them pass through a metal door to enter the tunnels. Dozens of lamps lit their way as they descended, following the sounds of raucous cheering.

Suddenly the narrow tunnel opened into a massive cave where three rings had been erected. A row of cells filled the farthest wall, and men huddled around the center ring where two men were boxing bare-knuckled.

"Good God," Graham muttered as one man knocked the other man's face so hard teeth went flying. "Phillip, let's go. It's not worth it. My brother Charles could help pay off your debts. I'm sure he won't mind—"

"No," Phillip said. "I incurred the debts, and I will pay them off." He would not dishonor his parents' memories by letting someone else save him.

"You and your bloody pride," Graham growled.

"If you don't approve, then leave," Phillip snapped, half hoping his friend would go so he wouldn't see what a damned mess this was going to be.

"I'm not leaving you," Graham promised.

Phillip moved toward a tall man in a top hat who seemed to be in charge of the fights. He carried a leather ledger under one arm.

"What do you want?" the man demanded as Phillip stood before him.

"I owe a debt to a Mr. Daniel Sheffield. I was told I could pay it off by fighting in one match."

The man's eyes widened ever so slightly, and a shrewd look replaced his surprise.

"Well now, that can be arranged. We have an opening now." The man pointed to the center ring, where the two men had ceased fighting. The smaller, weaker opponent lay on the ground, unmoving. The winner raised his fists and howled in triumph. Two men entered the ring and carried the fallen man's limp body away, dragging him behind them without respect or ceremony.

Phillip swallowed hard as he studied the man he was about to fight, the same man who'd just won the previous fight. He wore loose trousers and a white shirt made of cheap material. It was stained with blood. The man's knuckles were bloody as he curled them into meaty fists.

"Very well." Phillip removed his coat and gave it to Graham. "Graham, if..." He wasn't sure what he wanted to say, but he was glad his friend hadn't abandoned him.

"I have your back," Graham promised.

"Thank you." Phillip faced the ring and climbed

inside. The other man laughed and waved his hands at Phillip in open invitation.

"We got us a fancy one, eh?" he laughed.

Phillip was patient, having trained with the best boxers in Jackson's boxing club. He was prepared for an elegant match, but this? He knew the man before him would fight unfairly and quite possibly try to kill him.

I just need to survive, that's all.

Phillip was barely in the ring before the man charged him like a bull. Dodging back and to the side, he let the man stumble. But before Phillip could capitalize on that, the man was back up and charging at him again. The first blow to his jaw hurt like the devil, and he shook his head to clear the dizziness before he retaliated.

For several minutes it was a good series of blows between him and his opponent before Phillip realized he could guess the man's next moves. He started to block more effectively and respond with more power. His opponent was finally starting to tire out.

"C'mon! Kill the fancy tosser, Draper!" someone shouted from the crowd. The comment distracted Phillip, and he took a blow to his stomach.

"Take him down, Kent!" Graham's shout was the only one in his favor.

"Bloody hell!" Phillip launched himself at the man, tackling him to the ground. He swung his fist hard and broke the man's jaw. For a long second he thought the man would get up, but he slumped unconscious on the floor. Sweating hard, Phillip stepped off the man and started to exit the ring. Every muscle in him was quivering in the aftermath.

Two large men stepped up to block his path.

"I fought my battle and won. Mark it down for Daniel Sheffield. I paid his debt."

"Get back in there," one man growled. "The debt that he demands is your life."

"What?" Phillip searched the crowds for the man who kept the leather-bound ledger, but he was nowhere to be found.

"Kent!" Graham's warning cry came too late. He was knocked to the ground by someone and lost within the crowd.

He demands your life.

The words echoed in Phillip's mind as he fought for his life once more. But it still wasn't enough. After his next victory, they pitted him against three men at one time. He felt his left leg shatter beneath a kick and his ribs break as he fell to the ground.

Pain like he'd never known drowned out all other thoughts. Blood dripped into his eyes, coloring his world dark red. He saw Graham fighting to get to him. But the men in the room turned on Graham, beating him down again. Then everything went black.

❄

DEATH DIDN'T SEEM TO WISH TO CLAIM HIM, however. Phillip lay in that twilight world between life and death, his soul not firmly on either side. The shouts of the men faded into a heavy silence, and his body seized in pain until he was too weak to even shudder as his body tried to perish. He was going to die here in the shadows, where no one would find him and return him to the light.

Hours passed. Or was it days? He couldn't tell anymore. Then he heard a voice.

"There."

Hands were touching him, but his tongue was swollen and he couldn't make a sound as he was rolled onto his back.

"His leg has been broken," someone said. "What animals would do this and call it sport?" The voice was familiar, but he couldn't think past the pain.

"Graham said they beat him until he stopped moving."

Have to move, have to speak. Phillip summoned the last bit of his strength to move. He sucked in a lungful of air, stretching his broken ribs.

"Bloody Christ!" another voice gasped.

"He's not dead!"

Phillip moaned as he was lifted up.

"Phillip? Can you hear me?" the second voice demanded. He recognized that voice as well, but he was in too much pain to make sense of it.

"G—Graham..." Pain tore through him as he spoke.

"Graham sent me," the man said. "Good God, Ash. We've got to get him out."

Ash? Ashton Lennox? Good man, he thought before he slipped into darkness again.

He woke again sometime later and realized he wasn't moving. He was flat, on a cushioned bed.

"My lord, my name is Dr. Shreve. I'm here to inspect your injuries. If you are able, speak to me of any pain that you feel."

Phillip tried to speak, but his lips felt heavy, and he was still tongue-tied. The doctor must have noticed his sluggish struggles because he spoke up.

"It's all right if you can't talk. I'll give you something for the pain, which will help you rest. Once the swelling goes down on your face, we'll speak again."

Wishing he could move, could speak, Phillip struggled to make some noise, but something cool touched his lips. A rounded glass, a bottle? The sickly bittersweet taste of laudanum hit his tongue, and he flinched.

"Easy, my lord, this will help with the pain."

The liquid began to work quickly, but not before he heard the doctor speak to someone, though the conversation was muffled as though he stood outside the door.

"How is he?"

"He has several broken ribs, and his left leg is fractured in two places, but I'm most concerned about the injuries inflicted to his skull. I reset the leg and bound it, but the rest?" The doctor paused. "If he survives the next week, he may well yet recover, but it is in God's hands now."

Whatever else the doctor said was lost as Phillip faded into oblivion.

2

Ella was tired of being treated as though she were a fragile flower. Yes, she had been a weak child, always catching ill, but she hadn't been ill in years.

"Mother, I really wish to go to Lady Amelia's ball. She said that many handsome young men have been invited." She didn't add that she wasn't interested in any of them, but her mother might believe that and be more inclined to let her go.

Her mother paused in her reading of the *Morning Post* and sighed thoughtfully. "Dancing too much tires you out, my dear. I don't wish to put you at risk."

"I'm not made of spun glass. One dance will not shatter me."

"I distinctly remember that you had a coughing fit at the last one, only a month ago."

Ella rolled her eyes. "That wasn't my fault. Lady

Casterly smothered her entire body in some overripe eau de cologne. More than one person succumbed to a coughing fit when they found themselves within breathing distance of her. Lord Evanston even knocked over a tray of ratafia when he started coughing."

That particular moment had made her laugh and cough all the harder. Evanston was a handsome viscount and quite amusing. He'd been teasing her about Lady Casterly's overpowering scent before they both succumbed to it.

Her mother made a little sound of skepticism, and Ella closed her book. If she was to win this argument, she would need to be fully focused. Violet Humphrey was not an easy opponent.

"Mother, please, just listen to—"

The drawing room door burst open, and her eldest brother, Charles, strode inside. Her mother set her paper down so she could embrace her favorite child.

"Oh, Charles, my dear. What are you doing here?"

"I had to come see my mother and sister." He shot Ella a wink, and she found her irritation at being interrupted with their mother already fading. It was nearly impossible to stay mad at Charles. As the Earl of Lonsdale, he was a powerful peer, but as her brother, he was a frequent confidant, a surrogate father, and a dear friend. She knew that all of London was abuzz with his romantic entanglements, including his most recent scandal at Lord Sanderson's ball.

"Tell me the truth now," their mother demanded.

She fixed Charles with a sharp gaze honed by years of raising rogues for children.

"Truth? I have no idea what you're talking about," Charles answered.

Ella could see quite plainly he was lying. She had gotten very good at reading her two older brothers, especially when they were hiding the truth.

"There's a woman," their mother insisted.

Ella opened her book again but didn't turn any pages as she waited to hear how Charles would deflect her mother's inquiry. He was a notorious rogue, and no woman yet had captured his attention the way rumors around town now suggested. Their mother produced one of her fans and waved it in front of her face.

"There are plenty of women. You...Ella...the cook...," Charles teased their mother. Ella had to bite her lip to keep from laughing. She knew she ought not to encourage Charles's bad behavior.

"Plenty of women? Oh!" Violet snapped her fan shut and pointed the end at Charles the way a fencer would point a fencing foil.

"I believe London is full of women, or haven't you noticed?"

"Ella, fetch my smelling salts. Your brother is trying to kill me."

With a sigh, Ella set her book down and retrieved a tiny bottle from her reticule and held it out to her mother. Violet swatted her hand away.

"Not now. Wait until I actually faint," her mother hissed dramatically.

Charles grinned deviously at Ella and their mother. Violet narrowed her eyes.

"The girl at the Sandersons' ball. Who is she?" Violet demanded.

Ella perked up at the mention. She too wanted to know who the woman was. Charles had purposely caused all of the men on the young lady's dance card to have unfortunate accidents, preventing her from dancing with anyone but him the entire evening. He had never done that for any woman before.

"A girl now? Not a woman? I thought we were speaking of women? What interest would I possibly have in girls?"

Charles's words brought back a memory from a long-ago Christmas where she had foolishly thrown herself at Lord Kent. She had been a girl then, and he'd wanted nothing to do with her. The memory made her mind flood with disquieting thoughts of the past and the regrets she carried about that night. If only she hadn't asked for a kiss, they might have continued to play billiards, and she wouldn't have made such a fool of herself.

Their mother growled and chucked her fan at Charles, who deftly caught it.

"You know exactly what I mean, Charles Michael Edward Humphrey. Now talk."

"Oh," he sighed dramatically. "The girl from the Sandersons' ball. You must mean Lily Wycliff."

"Yes. That Wycliff girl. Who is she?"

Ella leaned closer. Whatever woman held his interest was certainly worth hearing about.

"Well, she's a widow." Charles's teasing tone turned more serious.

Violet's brows drew together. "A widow?"

"Her husband, Aaron Wycliff, was a favorite cousin of the Duchess of Essex."

"A country gentleman, then?" Her mother tapped her fingers against her chin in thought.

"I believe so," Charles answered, and Ella watched in fascination as her brother and mother seemed to have a silent conversation as well, spoken only in looks, as to how serious the situation was.

"And the widow? Where do her people hail from?"

Charles's mouth opened, but then he looked slightly baffled. "I honestly have no idea."

Ella set her book down and gave up all pretense of reading.

"You are falling in love with a woman, and you don't even know who she is?" Violet continued.

Ella was tempted to cut in and tell her mother that sometimes love at first sight did exist. She had experienced that once, years ago. Kent's soft eyes filled her mind before she banished the painful memory.

Charles frowned. "I didn't say I was falling in love with her. We've only just met."

Ella saw her brother's brow twitch, a sure indication he was lying. He was smitten by this mysterious widow. It was no surprise. Ella had heard her friends gossiping over tea yesterday about Charles and Lily Wycliff at the ball.

"You're in love, my dear boy," Violet sighed. "I've heard from more than one friend at the ball about how you looked at her and how she looked at you."

"Radiant, I believe someone said," Ella cut in. Her friend Lysandra Russell had told her about it. "Radiant. Charming. Buoyant. Though one person did say 'a couple of lovesick fools.'" That had also been from Lysandra, who had a rather negative view of love herself. Lysandra had no time for love, secretly pursuing a degree in the sciences at the moment with the help of the Society of Rebellious Ladies.

Her brother flushed and tugged at his neckcloth, and Ella bit her lip to hide a smile. It was always entertaining to provoke her brother.

"Yes, I heard that too," Violet agreed.

"I heard she has a child." This was also something of interest to Ella. Her brother had fallen for a woman with a child. Charles was good with children, but she never thought he would take to a woman who already had one.

"A child?" His mother's expression hardened. "That may be a problem."

Charles shot Ella an unamused expression. No doubt he had wanted to keep that bit of news a secret for a little while longer. She offered Charles an apologetic shrug while their mother was distracted.

"I don't see it as such. I would welcome her child as my own. If she will have me."

Her mother's face softened. "Well, if you will welcome the child, then so shall I. So it seems you have decided then? After all these years, you've found a woman worthy of your affections?"

Charles answered without hesitation. "Yes."

Joy blossomed in Ella's chest. She had longed for her brother to marry so that she might have a sister to bond with. Now she would have a sister and a niece or nephew.

"When shall we meet her?" Ella asked Charles.

"Er...I am taking her to the opera tonight."

Violet clapped her hands together. "Splendid! Ella and I shall accompany you and Mrs. Wycliff in your box. You shall meet us there."

The thought of going to the opera made Ella brighten. She'd have a chance to get out and enjoy the evening.

"Very good," Charles said, then cleared his throat. "Mother, has Graham written to you?"

"Graham? Not since last week. Why?"

The odd note of tension in Charles's tone caught Ella and Violet's attention.

"I must ask that you not overreact, Mother, but Graham was injured." Charles then rushed to assure his mother. "I've been taking care of him."

Ella clutched her closed book tightly in her hands. Something terrible had happened—she could see it in Charles's face. How had he managed to hide this so long? Her two brothers hadn't been close in years, and to hear that Charles was taking care of him only worried Ella further.

"Injured?" The word escaped from Violet's lips.

"He's healing and safe."

Their mother leapt to her feet. "Safe? What do you mean? Is he in danger?"

Ella held the book now in a white-knuckled grip as her mother started to panic.

Charles grasped her by her hands. "Mother, you really must sit. I will explain everything if you let me."

Their mother threw out a hand in Ella's direction. "Smelling salts, now!" Ella desperately searched for the bottle again and pressed it into her mother's hands. Rather than use the bottle, her mother tossed it against the wall and crossed her arms over her chest, glowering at Charles.

"You will talk, *now*, dear boy."

Charles audibly swallowed and shot Ella a pleading look, but Ella was the last person to stand in between their mother and anyone. Violet was a fierce creature when provoked.

"Graham and Lord Kent were gambling. Kent had an unusually poor streak," Charles began. Ella gasped at the mention of Lord Kent's name.

"What happened?" Her heart leapt into her throat at the thought that Phillip was involved.

"Kent was given the chance to fight in a boxing ring to pay off his debts, but in the process, he was gravely injured. Graham tried to help him, but they beat him as well. But Graham is going to be fine."

The world seemed to start to blur around Ella, and she heard a faint ringing in her ears. Phillip was hurt. She could see it in Charles's eyes. Whatever had happened was bad, very, very bad.

"Thank God," their mother said and brushed away a few tears.

"And Lord Kent?" Ella's heart pounded hard deep within her chest.

"He will be all right...I hope. The doctor said if he can survive a few weeks, he will pull through."

Charles's words echoed dully inside her head. Phillip was hurt badly enough that he could die.

No. He couldn't die. She wouldn't let him. As foolish as it was, she'd never gotten over him, and she'd never forgotten that night in the billiard room so many years ago when he'd broken her heart. Nor had she forgotten the second kiss he'd stolen the night of her debut. The man seemed to mark the milestones in her life with kisses and heartache. But it didn't change how she felt. She was still in love with him.

"May I go see him?" she asked, then realized she couldn't let her brother know she meant Lord Kent. He might tell her no. "I mean Graham, of course. But also Lord Kent."

Her brother raised one brow. "I suppose, if Mother doesn't object."

Ella looked pleadingly at her mother.

"As long as you aren't underfoot while Charles is pursuing Mrs. Wycliff. Lord knows your brother will need every advantage to win this woman."

Ella couldn't believe her mother had brushed aside Lord Kent's condition and even Graham's so easily. But it was in her mother's nature to bury worry and pain deep.

"I won't," Ella replied at the same time Charles said, "She won't."

"Then you must go," Violet said. "Graham is truly well?"

"Yes, a bit bruised, but he will be fine," Charles assured their mother, but Ella saw the lie. Graham was more than a bit bruised.

"But he came to you? Of all places? Does that mean...?" Violet's eyes brightened with hope.

Ella looked at Charles as well. Graham and Charles rarely spoke, except during the holidays. She knew it was because Graham blamed Charles for their father's death. But their father had died of a stroke. It wasn't Charles's fault.

Charles cupped Violet's shoulders. "I think so, yes. He is still cautious, but that is only natural under the circumstances. I, for my part, will do all I can to make amends while he is under my roof."

Violet wiped at her eyes. "That's wonderful. You know how much it has broken my heart to see you two not speaking to each other."

"I know. But it will still take time."

Ella agreed. Charles and Graham's division had hurt everyone. Graham had spent much time away from them. Lord Kent had been and still was Graham's closest friend, and Ella was thankful that her brother had Lord Kent in his life—at least until today. They had both been reckless and foolish.

Violet wiped her eyes again. "Well, let's focus on this evening. The opera and meeting your Mrs. Wycliff. We shall see you tonight then, dear boy."

Ella stood frozen by her chair as Charles left. She didn't want to go to the opera. She wanted to be with Phillip, to see him.

"Mother, may I go and visit Graham this afternoon?"

"Hmm?" Her mother was distracted too. "Oh...yes. Go on, my dear. I will visit Graham this evening before the opera."

Ella slipped out of the room and rushed upstairs to change into a walking dress. She had no intention of waiting any longer than she had to. She would go at once.

"I'm coming, Phillip. Please hold on."

❧ 3 ❧

Ella arrived at Charles's townhouse two hours later, hastily thanking his butler, Mr. Ramsey.

"Good afternoon, Ramsey. I've come to see my brother and Lord Kent."

The butler nodded. "This way. His lordship mentioned you may come by," Mr. Ramsey replied, and his eyes deepened with concern. "Your brother and Lord Kent are resting upstairs. Which do you prefer to see first?"

"My brother," she added, and Ramsey showed her to an upstairs chamber. Graham was sleeping, but Ramsey assured her that the doctor had said he would be better in a few days.

"I must warn you, Miss Humphrey, Lord Kent is in a bad way, a very bad way indeed. Best to brace yourself."

"Thank you." She followed him to another bedroom. The room was dark, but a few lamps had been lit. Ella's

37

heart skipped a beat as she glimpsed a figure lying on the bed.

"Is there anything I can do for him?" she asked.

"Be with him," Mr. Ramsey said. "Just let him feel your presence. The doctor told us that if he can survive the week, he'll likely heal in time, but there's a concern about bleeding on his brain."

Ella slowly approached the bed. "And his other injuries?"

"His left leg was badly broken. The doctor said it will heal, but he'll most likely have a limp. He suffered a few broken ribs as well."

Ella covered her mouth with a trembling hand. It was all so much worse than she had feared.

"If you want, you could apply a cool cloth to his forehead. Perhaps get him to drink a bit of water. That might help." The butler pointed to a pitcher of water and a glass as well as some fresh cloths.

"Thank you," she murmured to Ramsey before she approached the bed.

A chair had been placed at Phillip's bedside. Ella moved a little closer before she wet a clean cloth and placed it to his brow. His beautiful face had been transformed by black bruises and dried blood. She almost didn't recognize him.

"Oh, Phillip," she whispered. She was going to stay here as long as it took. She would not abandon him. She wasn't a child of fifteen anymore. Their paths had rarely crossed in the last five years, but that made little difference to her now. She still felt wildly nervous around him and dizzy in a way she'd never felt around any other man. Yet to see this tall, powerful, elegant, and sensual man brought so low, so wounded, it tore at her heart.

"Phillip, you must stay strong, do you hear me? You must survive." She washed away some dried blood from his lips. As she inspected the rest of his body, she discovered his knuckles were bloody and raw. She set the cloth aside and rang for a maid to bring her some salve. Once she had it, she dabbed her fingertips into the pot and carefully worked it into the cuts and broken skin of his knuckles, then his split lip and the cuts upon his brow.

Sometime later, she was exhausted and laid her head down to rest, only to jerk awake when he made a sound. It was somewhere between a groan and a mutter.

"Phillip?" She was careful to touch his arm where she knew it was not bruised.

He made the same sound again, like a moan deep at the back of his throat.

"How about a bit of water?" She filled the glass and held it to his lips. He managed a few tiny sips before he turned his head away, just a fraction. Ella's eyes blurred with tears, but she felt hopeful too.

"I'm here. I won't leave you." She brushed his dark hair back from his brow. "You're safe now. Dream and rest."

❄

THE VOICE OF AN ANGEL DRIFTED THROUGH THE PAIN.

"Dream and rest."

It made him feel safe enough to let himself go deeper into the realm of dreams, because he knew he would dream of her...

TWO YEARS AGO

Phillip lounged against a pillar at the back of the assembly room in London, watching a crowd of debutantes being presented to the king. The elaborate affair happened only once a year, and all the eligible young ladies who'd come out for the year were presented to him, wearing their best white gowns.

"Lord, this nonsense drives a man to drink," Graham muttered next to him.

Phillip laughed at the expression on his friend's face. Graham mimed hanging himself with his neckcloth, and Phillip snorted. Two plump matrons with gigantic ostrich feathers in their turbans turned to scowl at them both.

"Hush!" one woman hissed, the jowls at her throat shaking with fury.

Phillip smacked Graham in the chest to silence him, otherwise Graham would have choked on his laughter. Phillip had always had a healthy respect for ladies in society, especially those with daughters of marriageable age. If a man was not cautious around them, they would find a way to ensnare him in a compromising position with their daughter. Society dictated a gentleman was to pursue a lady, yet everyone also knew that many rich, titled men like himself tended not to give chase, which made quite a few matchmaking mamas desperate.

Graham had little to fear from such women. As the younger brother to the Earl of Lonsdale, he did not attract much focus, which suited Graham just fine. He preferred to chase lusty young widows and had turned that into an art form. But Phillip was not so inclined. He had not found a woman yet to attract his attention.

No, that wasn't entirely true. There had been one woman, one he'd kept a safe distance from for three years.

"Ah, there she is. Little bit's all grown up." Graham sighed and nodded at the young lady currently curtsying to the king. Phillip's heart stopped.

Ella wore a cream-colored gown embroidered with pale gold thread in the shape of flying swallows. The lamplight gleamed favorably on the crown of her gold hair, and the loose locks had been pulled back into a Grecian style. Gold satin ribbons were threaded through her hair as a sort of headband. Jewels glinted off the ribbon, calling more attention to her hair and face.

Her features were delicate, her mouth full and her eyes almost slumberous, as though she had lived all of her life in the midst of a wonderful dream. Her chin was a little square, but the strength it gave her features did not detract from her femininity. Her porcelain skin was slightly rosy along her cheekbones as she blushed when the king nodded in approval. A few loose tendrils bounced down against her cheeks as she bent her head before straightening and standing aside for the next young woman to be presented.

"Ella," Graham called out to his sister, jolting Phillip back to self-awareness as well as earning fresh scowls from the two women in front of them.

"Sorry, quite sorry," Graham replied smoothly, trying to unruffle their feathers. Then Graham waved at his sister, who joined them. Her face was still flushed with excitement, and Phillip bit the inside of his cheek to keep his body from responding to her. He couldn't afford to do or say anything foolish with most of the *ton* watching them. Yet he couldn't resist wondering if that was how she would look in bed beneath him after he'd given her the most exquisite pleasure.

"You did well, Ella. Mama is beaming with pride." Graham kissed her forehead. Ella's gaze darted to Phillip. Her sweet, searching, yet bold gaze made his blood hum with forbidden desire.

"Yes, you did very well," Phillip found himself adding.

He had done his best to stay away from her after that night in the billiard room three years ago. But in that time, she had grown from a very young lady of fifteen to a grown woman of eighteen. Her curvy figure was both regal and elegant, and there was even a delicate nature about her—not one of the body, but of the spirit.

No...that wasn't quite right. He had trouble trying to put into words what it was that called upon every protective instinct within him.

Her blue-gray eyes were locked on his, their slightly tilted shape making her appear a little more exotic and the hopeful twinkle in them a tad impish. That was it. She made him think of a fae princess, delicate in appearance, but surprisingly strong. Yet at the same time, one word of disapproval or disappointment from someone she trusted would crush her. A delicate heart, but only toward those she loved. To all others, she was a bastion of inner strength.

The music changed in the room as the presentation ended.

"Now for the dances," Graham said, and he gave Phillip an appraising look. "Take my place and dance with Ella for me? Lord Garnsey's widow has just arrived." Graham grinned in greeting at a buxom brunette in a deep-red dress who had just walked into the assembly room.

Before either Ella or Phillip could stop him, Graham had slipped away through the crush of people, leaving Phillip alone with the woman he desperately wanted to bed and also needed to avoid.

"You don't have to dance with me, Lord Kent. I would not hold you to that. I will find the other ladies without partners." She turned to join a group of young women who had all gathered forlornly at the far wall. The thought of Ella joining them, her disappointment mingling with theirs, made him act. He reached out and caught her wrist.

"Wait, I will claim your first dance. Allow the men here a chance to see what they are missing." Her slender wrist was warm in his hand, and his pulse beat faster as he led her out onto the center of the floor.

Three couples joined him and Ella to form a rectangle for a quadrille. As they began, Phillip let go of his reservations and gave in to his delight in dancing with her. Graham and Charles always said she was fragile, like a flower that had bloomed too early and one good frost could destroy her delicate bloom, but Phillip saw none of that. He saw only a woman with the light of joy in her eyes. She laughed as they spun and moved apart and back together, and soon the other couples were smiling too. Her genuine joy of the moment was infectious.

When the dance ended, his heart sank and he led her back to the side of the ballroom where her mother and eldest brother, Charles, stood.

"Lonsdale," he said to Charles. Despite Graham and Charles's distance between each other, Phillip had maintained a steady friendship with Charles over the years.

"Kent, well done. Ella seemed to enjoy that." Charles offered his younger sister a benevolent smile.

Ella slowly pulled her arm free of Phillip's and lowered her head to hide a fresh blush.

"Where the devil is Graham?" Charles asked Ella. "Wasn't he supposed to dance with you?"

Phillip replied for her. "He needed to catch a bit of air, I believe." The little white lie kept Ella from appearing abandoned by her own brother in favor of a busty widow.

"Ah." Charles frowned slightly, perhaps seeing through the deception, and then smiled at Ella. "My turn, little bit." He offered her his arm and escorted her back onto the dance floor. Phillip remained next to the dowager countess.

"Thank you for sparing Ella being left out of her first dance. I will have a word with Graham when he resurfaces."

"My pleasure. Ella is a lovely young woman," he replied, his gaze still on her as she danced with Charles.

Violet watched her daughter with pride. "She is, isn't she? She was so sick as a young child, the way children are when born too early, but she turned out quite well."

Phillip couldn't help but agree. Ella Humphrey was an exquisite woman, the kind who would age with timeless beauty, much like her mother. But looks weren't the only thing that mattered, at least not to Phillip. His parents had been a love match, and he had been raised in a home that showed what love could be like. And Phillip would only love a woman who was more beautiful on the inside than the outside. His father used to say that a woman's heart and mind would be his truest and dearest companions when the years turned him old and gray. Beauty of the body faded, but not beauty of the heart or mind.

Ella spun around the dance floor, her bell-like laughter stirring something deep inside him, an old ache for things he had buried since his parents had died. It almost hurt to watch her natural joy.

"Please excuse me, my lady." He bowed to Violet and left the room. He stepped into the moonlit gardens at the back of the assembly rooms. It was September, and the leaves had turned to red and gold. The light bite of the winter chill hung upon the air, promising an early frost. He enjoyed the fall, the way he could smell the coming of winter and feel strangely alive.

Fall brought out a melancholy feeling in him with each day that passed. Bittersweet thoughts of summers gone before seemed to deepen his understanding of the world and his fellow man.

He moved off the marble steps and went deeper into the gardens, only to stumble as someone bumped into him from behind. He turned, catching the person as they fell into his chest.

"Oh, excuse me!" A sweet, almost husky voice tightened his body with hunger as he recognized the voice.

"Ella?" He spoke her given name, then nearly bit his tongue before he corrected himself. "Lady Ella?"

"Phillip?" Ella gasped and corrected herself as well. "I mean, Lord Kent."

"No, please, call me Phillip." He made sure she was steady before he released her.

"Well, if that is what you wish, then you must call me Ella." She smiled up at him, and her eyes reflected the nearly full moon far above them. She trembled a little. The expanse of her ivory skin exposed along her neck and shoulders no doubt let her become more chilled than him.

"Are you cold, Ella?" He couldn't resist speaking her name. He liked the way it rolled sweetly off his tongue.

"A little. I was dreadfully warm inside, and yet I take one step out here and I'm suddenly cold. How silly."

He grinned down at her, even knowing he was playing with fire by standing this close. "Not silly at all." He removed his coat and swung it around her shoulders, pulling it closed in front of her like a cloak. She was dwarfed by it and looked so small and delicate. Seeing her in his clothes appealed to some primal need inside him. He nearly laughed at the thought that a civilized gentleman of the modern age would feel like one of his ancient ancestors by showing he could care for his woman. He was distracted by the way the moonlight seemed to illuminate her dark-gold lashes as she gazed up at him.

Lord, she is beautiful.

"Thank you, Phillip." She snuggled more deeply into his coat. "Did I disturb you just now? If so, I'm terribly sorry."

"No, not at all. I like to take a bit of air myself."

She nodded and then looked away shyly. "Thank you for dancing with me. I truly didn't wish to join the other wallflowers, not at my first ball."

"Nor should you have. It was shameful for Graham to leave you like that, but I confess it was my delight to benefit from his absence." He wanted to court her, wanted to be the man to lay claim to her heart, but he'd already suffered such great pain, such loss. He wasn't sure he could go through it again. It was better not to love, even as irresistible as she was.

Ella was looking at him again, and her blue-gray eyes seemed to strip him bare, rocking him clear down to his very bones.

"You were kind to me all those years ago," she said suddenly. "I didn't understand then why you were, but I do now."

Those penetrating eyes held him prisoner. He couldn't look away.

He was confused. "Kind?"

"In the billiard room. I was young, too young to understand that what I asked of you was dangerous. I was a foolish girl." Now she looked away, breaking eye contact, and suddenly he could breathe again.

"Oh" was all he found the strength to say.

"I wanted to thank you, that is all. I don't wish for any more awkwardness between us." She laughed, the sound sweet and almost teasingly impish. "I'm sure I could find another man to kiss me now that I'm grown."

She tilted her face up at the moon, so calm and self-assured.

Phillip was awestruck. In many ways she hadn't changed, not in the ways that mattered. The girl who'd helped him forget his sorrows that night three years ago, however briefly, was still there, but that only made her more tempting. She was indeed grown. A woman's mind, a woman's heart, and now she was out in society, seeking kisses from men who might not have the self-control he had had three years ago.

"Ella, surely you know that most men are dangerous. You cannot go about asking for kisses. You could be compromised and find yourself married to some fool who won't..." He swallowed the rest of his words, too afraid to let her hear what was in his mind.

"Who won't what?"

He raised a hand to her head, curling his fingers around the neck that he could spend hours exploring with his lips. Her slender hands twisted in her skirts, yet she held still except to lift her head up, angling her lips closer to his.

"What?" she repeated, but he had already forgotten whatever he'd been about to say as he fixated on those lips. They reminded him of fresh rose blooms, and he imagined they would taste as soft and sweet as they looked.

"A man who won't appreciate you for the gift you are," he said, his body dangerously close to taking control.

Her dark-gold brows arched mischievously. "Then I must find a man who is not dangerous, I suppose. Would you...kiss me? Now that I am grown?"

Not dangerous...hardly. Phillip felt like he was back in the billiard room, trying to remember that he was a good man, not some bloody rakehell who would take advantage of a sweet young woman. But damned if Ella didn't seem to find every chink in his armor and crawl underneath. He struggled to remember that he was a gentleman as he was swept away by the magnetic compulsion of Ella's moonlit eyes.

"If I kiss you, then you must let no other man do this unless you intend to marry him. Others would seek to take advantage of you."

"You will be my tutor, then?" Images flashed through his mind of her in his bed, exhausted and happy after hours of lovemaking.

"Just this once," he breathed, every muscle in him straining against his fraying control.

"One kiss? But I couldn't possibly learn enough from just one," she teased, her voice gentle as a caress.

"You'd be surprised, darling." He couldn't resist smiling at her.

He took her hand and led her deeper into the gardens. They found a marble bench a few turns in, and after making sure they were alone, he pulled her down to the bench beside him. He had but one brief second to think clearly, to change his mind, but then she placed one hand over his thigh and he was lost.

"A kiss sometimes begins soft," he murmured as he leaned down and cupped her face in his hands. She closed her eyes as he brushed his lips back and forth over hers. They were even softer than he had imagined.

"Can it be hard?" she asked against his mouth.

"Yes, my darling, it can, but that comes later. Part your lips—let me explore you."

She opened her lips, and he playfully licked at her with his tongue before he slid it inside to touch hers. She jolted against him, and he bound an arm around her waist, holding her close.

"This is how the French kiss," he said. "Slow. Intimate." She gave a shivery sigh as her tongue sought entrance to his mouth this time. Lord, he could become drunk on Ella and her kisses. Simply having her in his arms was making his senses spin.

"I like it," she whispered back. He smiled and bit her bottom lip, drawing it deeper into his mouth before he let go and released it. He slid his hands down her back to caress her bottom and couldn't resist squeezing it. She whimpered and leaned into him even more. This time when he kissed her, he kissed hard, devouring her with his mouth, relishing her little gasps of shock and delight as he conquered her with kisses.

He moved fast, lifting her up so she sat across his lap. It gave him better access to her legs and her dainty ankles. He slid one hand up her skirts, drawing his fingertips along her calf over her white stockings. Her breath hitched, and she curled her arms around his neck.

"I feel so strange," she said.

"You do? Where, my love?" he asked, trying not to smile as he realized she was becoming aroused, possibly for the first time.

"My lower belly..." She sounded surprised.

"That's desire, darling." He continued to stroke her calf, noting with pride the little tremors that came from her as she started to shift restlessly on his lap.

"You feel that way too?" She caressed the back of his neck, lightly running her nails through his hair at the base of his skull. She was a pure delight.

"I do, especially when you do that." He shuddered as she continued that delicious friction through his hair, and a bolt of fiery need shot straight through him.

"What is—?" She rolled her hips on top of his lap, clearly feeling him harden beneath her.

"Sorry, my darling. I cannot seem to control my reactions to you."

"Oh. This is normal?" She seemed puzzled by what she'd felt.

"It is."

She lowered her head, slowly kissing him again, and her wanton sighs and feverous kisses helped convince him that perhaps he had died and was now in heaven.

Voices in the garden drew close, too close. It was like a splash of cold water on his head, jerking him back to reality.

"I think it's time we stopped. You must return to the ball before someone misses you." He gave her surprised lips one last lingering kiss before he set her off his lap. She straightened her skirts, and they both walked back to the entrance to the assembly rooms.

"Go on," he urged when she tried to take him back in with her.

"You're not coming?" she asked.

"No, darling. I must be going home. Congratulations on your come-out." He cupped her cheek once more and brushed the pad of his thumb over her lips.

Then he stepped back and walked away. Leaving her behind created an ache in his chest, but he had done the right thing. If he had stayed, Ella would have been truly compromised. Graham and Charles would have demanded he marry her. Marriage in and of itself was not the problem, but losing Graham's trust and possibly his friendship was not something he could survive. Nor could he trust his heart to another soul again only to have it shattered forever if he dared to love Ella and then lost her.

❧ 4 ❧

Phillip hurt everywhere. There was not one bit of muscle, sinew, or bone that didn't ache, tighten, or scream in agony. His thoughts were broken, mere fragments as a pulse pounded inside his throbbing skull. He tried to speak, but the breath in his lungs was too shallow. His limbs were like dead weights at his sides as he fought in vain to move, even an inch in any direction.

What happened? What...?

He struggled to catch hold of his last memories.

Cards...wagers...tunnels...blood.

He'd lost a wager to a man and agreed to fight in the Lewis Street tunnels...and he'd been attacked, *outnumbered* and beaten near to death.

"Rest now. You're safe." A soft voice drifted through his head. A sweet scent filled his nose. A familiar scent...

"Help..." The word was barely a rasp.

"Are you thirsty?" the voice asked.

He tried to nod, but his head throbbed. Only a whimper escaped his lips.

"Don't move. The doctor said you must rest. Here, take some water." A glass was pressed to his mouth, and he sighed as cool water trickled between his lips and down his throat. Christ, it felt good just to have this meager relief.

"I prepared some chicken broth. Would you like to try it?" the voice asked, almost pleading with him.

This time he managed to nod. Though the motion was almost imperceptible, it was hellishly painful. He had only vague memories of rejecting food earlier and crying silently as he wished for death in order to escape the pain. That must have been real and not a dream. He didn't feel nauseated at that moment, so he parted his lips, and a spoon dribbled warm chicken broth into his mouth. He waited, expecting to toss his accounts, but the taste of the broth was actually good, so he opened his mouth again.

When she had finished, he sighed, his stomach full. And though it hurt his ribs, he felt better. So much better. A cool cloth was placed on his brow, and much of the tightness in his body eased.

"Sleep," the voice commanded. "Don't worry, I won't leave you."

He obeyed that sweet voice and drifted away.

After what seemed like ages, where he marked the passage of time only by being helped to eat, the puffy stinging in his face began to fade and he felt his eyelids begin to flutter. Soon he would be able to open his eyes and see.

"How is he today?" a deeper voice asked. Another familiar voice. They were friends. He was safe among friends.

"Much better. His face is barely swollen anymore. I was afraid they had broken his cheek or jaw, but now I think perhaps not." That sweet feminine voice, the voice of an angel, spoke clearly but softly. It was a voice that brought a great flood of joy through him. He wanted to open his eyes, to lay eyes upon his savior, but he couldn't. Despair would have choked him, but he knew that he would be all right so long as *she* was there.

The man chuckled. "Kent's head is as hard as a rock. There is no way they hurt him that badly."

"Oh, Graham, hush. This isn't amusing," the woman said. "We almost lost him—we almost lost *you*." The woman's tone sharpened as she chastised his best friend. He recognized Graham now, but so much was still hazy.

"I know, I'm sorry, Ella. I've been sick over all of this."

Ella? Who's Ella?

"I should never have let him go to the tunnels. Charles and I could have paid off the debt for him, but he wouldn't let us." Graham's tone softened a little.

Ella huffed, and for some reason the sound made Phillip want to smile. When she continued to speak, her voice was colored with melancholy and a hint of frustration.

"If men could learn to forgo their matters of pride, many a woman would be spared such heartache." There was a pause and a cough from Graham, and the woman continued. "Graham, you should still be in bed! You're barely better than Phillip. Don't make me send for Charles."

Flashes of Graham in the tunnels, fighting to get to him, screaming his name before he vanished beneath a tide of fists. Why couldn't he remember more beyond the cards and the tunnels? It was as though his life had been reduced to that one single memory, and all the pain in his body was tied to it.

"Fine, fine. I surrender. Lord, Ella, you're worse than Mother. She was already lecturing me on a dozen types of tea I should be drinking to reduce my pain and swelling." The pair of voices, Graham and the woman, were the only comfort to him. Their exasperation and teasing in turns was a light in a vast storm threatening to crash him upon a rocky shore.

The woman suddenly laughed, and the bell-like sound sent Phillip's heart racing. The blood now roaring into his head made him groan.

"Go on, Graham, you woke him up," the woman admonished.

"I'm sorry, Ella," Graham apologized.

Ella... He remembered now. Ella, who'd kissed him with such wild abandon and made a man forget his pain.

How could he ever have forgotten her? She was here? She was the one taking care of him? His angel, the woman who'd pulled him from the edge of death, was Graham's little sister, the woman he'd done his best to avoid because she was such a temptation.

Her words to Graham sank in, now colliding with his memories of Graham being beaten when he'd tried to rescue him. Phillip struggled to speak.

"Hush, Phillip, don't speak. You're all right. Rest."

What he wanted more than anything was to be able to open his eyes and see her. But his strength soon waned, and he slipped back into sleep.

Rain lashing on the windows and the chill of night woke him much later with shivers. Ella placed an extra blanket over him and murmured sweet words of comfort.

Sometime later, when the rain had ended and a fire was crackling in the room, he finally had the strength to open his eyes. Morning light bathed the room, almost blinding him. His first glimpse of Ella was hazy; she lay in a chair beside the bed, her body bent forward in an uncomfortable position as she rested her folded arms on the bed beside him.

She'd fallen asleep clasping one of his hands. Her fingers were warm, and he gave them a small squeeze. Motes of dust danced in the light, like shimmering flakes of snow that fell lightly into the golden crown of her hair. The silken strands were unbound and fell in loose waves down her shoulders. He moved his hand, slipping it free of her hold so he could touch her hair. He stroked it, then spooled it around one finger and stared at it in the light as she slowly woke.

For a time they gazed at each other, no words spoken between them, but he felt her searching his face, looking for answers.

"Phillip?" She gently caught his wrist as his hand began to fall. She held the back of his hand to her cheek, her blue-gray eyes spilling with fresh tears.

"Ella." He sighed her name as a sense of comfort swept over him. He hadn't been dreaming. She was really here looking after him.

"I'm here. Are you thirsty? Hungry?" She leaned closer, a floral scent teasing his nose. Lord, he could breathe that scent for years and never tire of it.

He found it a little easier to speak now. "What happened?"

Ella offered him some water. "Graham escaped the tunnels. He was badly hurt, but able to walk. He came to Charles. He thought you were dead, but he begged Charles to find you."

"And he did. I remember...I thought it was Graham at first." He puzzled over the blurry memories in his mind. "Was Lennox there as well?"

Ellen nodded. "They saved you. I've been here looking after you for almost two weeks now."

"So long...?" Phillip stared at her for a moment, wanting to tell her the truth. That he had been nearly ready to die, but hearing her voice, feeling her touch, had been what saved him. "Thank you for caring for me," he said quietly, but he knew she heard him. She tightened her hold on his hand and nodded.

"I would do anything for you," she said. Then her lashes fanned down, and she blushed. In the morning light, her skin looked like alabaster kissed by a pale rose. She was so lovely to look upon that it hurt. But unlike his current condition, it was a pain he gladly embraced.

"Should I fetch Dr. Shreve? He was most anxious to hear the moment you woke up."

Phillip nodded. It would be best if she left for a bit. He needed time. Time to remind himself that he had to guard his heart and not let her past his walls. She exited the room, and with her went all of his joy. Even the sunlight seemed less golden as it washed over the bed and the furniture around him. Closing his eyes, he rested for a bit, but a sound soon woke him. Graham was sitting in the chair Ella had vacated.

"You're awake, thank Christ," Graham said. His face was a red-and-purple collage of bruises, still quite swollen.

"You look like hell," he said to his friend, earning a pained chuckle from Graham.

"And you look far worse."

"Of that I have no doubt." Phillip cracked a small smile. Graham looked down at his boots, and his shoulders sagged.

"I failed you, Phillip. I'm sorry. I shouldn't have let you go in there."

Phillip reached for Graham's arm and patted it. "You didn't fail me. I failed myself. I was stubborn. My damned pride. But you got out and found help. I am thankful beyond words to call you my friend."

Graham sniffed and wiped his nose like a child, and Phillip was stunned by his friend's reaction. "You're my best friend," Graham whispered hoarsely. "You were there for me when my father died all those years ago."

"And you were there for me when my parents died," Phillip reminded him. His own heart swelled with a whirl of emotions—pride, love, honor, and embarrassment. But he was too tired to keep his usual reserve.

"Go on and sleep. Ella is happy to play the nursemaid." Graham laughed. But Phillip knew he wouldn't be laughing if he ever knew how much Phillip cared for her. Phillip closed his eyes again and listened drowsily as Graham shuffled out of the bedroom.

"I swear, Graham, if you don't get some rest—" Ella growled from the direction of the door.

"I'm going, dear sister. Lord, you're becoming a battle-ax in your old age."

"I'm younger than you!" Ella protested.

Phillip's lips twitched into a smile as he drifted off to sleep.

❅

THE NEXT WEEK PASSED QUICKLY, TOO QUICKLY IN some ways. Ella was overjoyed at Phillip's progress, but she was afraid of what would happen when he was well enough to return to his estate. Soon her time of caring for him would be over, and they would go back to being people who'd shared a kiss once, a kiss that she'd wanted to build her life upon. And all he would see her as was someone who'd nursed him back to health. She didn't want gratitude—she wanted love, deep, passionate, life-altering love.

As she entered his bedchamber carrying a pitcher of water as she'd done dozens of times, without knocking, a privilege many women would envy, she gasped as she came upon him half-naked. His valet, Marcus, was helping him dress.

"Oh!" She froze, too shocked to know what to do next. "I'm so sorry."

Phillip gave a chuckle and fell back on his bed, still shirtless. "Marcus was bringing me a fresh shirt. Give us a moment."

The mere sight of him being so wonderfully, scandalously indecent made her turn hastily back toward the door as she tried to forget the sight she'd just witnessed —not that she ever could. Even so wounded, he was handsome. All that hard muscle and his broad shoulders and...heavens, she was thinking with her body like a silly debutante. She wasn't that girl anymore; she was a rational, sensible woman, not swayed by a perfect masculine form.

She dared not look over her shoulder, and continued to clutch a fresh pitcher of water, her face flaming.

"I'm so pleased to see you up. Well, sitting up, I mean." She could have smacked herself for how silly she sounded. But she couldn't deny the fear that once he was healed, he'd go back to his life and she'd go back to the proverbial shelf.

"All done," Phillip promised. "You may turn around now." When she turned, she saw he had changed clothes. He'd worn only drawers beneath the blankets, or so the doctor had said, since his broken leg was in need of constant watch for infection. But he'd needed to change his shirts frequently as he sweated through them. The valet bowed respectfully and departed. Ella waited for him to leave before she spoke.

She held up the pitcher. "I...er...brought fresh water, in case you were thirsty." She certainly was, her mouth ran dry whenever she looked at him.

Phillip's lips twitched in that almost-grin that made her knees weak. "Thank you, I am quite thirsty."

She cleared her throat and straightened her shoulders. "And I thought I could bring a bit of luncheon to you today? The kitchen has made some cold cuts and raspberry tarts."

Phillip's eyes lit up. "I am rather hungry." Then he scowled. "But I'm bloody sick of being trapped in this bed."

"I know. It must be so frustrating." She set the pitcher down on the washstand and poured him a glass. He accepted it, but his expression was marred with a sudden frown.

"How is Graham?" he asked.

"Better than you and just as grumpy," Ella replied a little tersely.

"I'm not grumpy," Phillip shot back.

"You most certainly are." Ella placed her hands on her hips and stared at him evenly until he grumbled an apology. "Dr. Shreve brought a Bath chair over for you to use." She went into the hall to retrieve the rolling chair and wheeled it in so he could see.

"That's for invalids," Phillip countered.

"Yes, and right now, it will let you have a bit of fresh air." Ella pushed it up to the bed next to him. "Do you want to try? Charles agreed to push you around in it."

Phillip stared at the chair for a long moment.

"At least you'll be outside this room," Ella prodded.

Finally he nodded. "All right."

Ella went outside and called for Charles. Then she waited outside while her brother helped Phillip into the chair and wheeled him into the corridor.

"Where to, Kent?" Charles asked with a chuckle. Phillip's face was ruddy with embarrassment as he looked to Ella.

"The library. I have an indoor picnic set up." She moved ahead of them to reach the library first so she could open the doors. Charles rolled Phillip up to the long reading table, which had been cleared of books and was now decorated with an assortment of cold cuts, a tray of tarts, and a tin of biscuits with a bit of wine.

She kissed her brother's cheek. "Thank you, Charles."

"Behave yourself now, Kent," Charles warned with a chuckle, and then he left them alone.

"Thank you, Ella," Phillip said quietly. "I was afraid I would never escape that bed."

She prepared him a plate of food and then one for herself. "I'm happy to help."

"I'm surprised you aren't busy planning a Christmas ball," Phillip said between bites. "The balls here used to be a part of your family tradition."

"They still are," she said with some melancholy. "But things are...*tense* at the moment. Yes, I suppose that's the right word. Charles is trying to convince Mother and me to visit our friends in Scotland, but I refuse to go while you and Graham require attention."

"Graham and I will be fine. We don't need to be watched by a mother hen."

Ella cut a sharp gaze at him. That wasn't she'd been called that by her brothers and she didn't like it now when Phillip said it. "I'm *not* a mother hen."

Phillip sighed and leaned back in the Bath chair. "I only meant that you care for others too much and barely at all for yourself." He opened his eyes. The sunny warmth of the library made his blue eyes bright and revealed the russet strands in his dark hair.

"I suppose it's because my family had to care for me when I was younger. I was quite ill most of my early youth."

"But you aren't anymore?" Phillip asked.

"No, I'm not, though my family still sometimes requires convincing."

"Then go and live your life. You should be at balls, finding a man who will worship you and—"

She waited for him to finish, but only silence came. "And?"

"Move on," Phillip finally said. "You let life freeze you in place, Ella."

For some reason, his words cut her deeply. She wasn't frozen. Was she?

She'd been waiting, waiting for Phillip to finally see her as a woman, but even now he was still treating her like a child. Even after that night in the garden two years ago. She got to her feet and walked over to the windows, smoothing her rose-colored skirts as she watched snow fall thick and white on the gardens. Her stomach knotted, and she felt that if she dared to move, she'd toss her accounts.

"I think I should return to my room and rest. The doctor should be by to visit shortly," Phillip said. His words were a dagger to her heart.

She swallowed her pride and her hurt as she turned to help him. He shook his head and moved his hands on the wheels, pushing himself. That only made her despair deepen.

"I'll have Marcus help me." He wheeled to the door and pulled the bell cord, which brought Marcus to him. The valet gave Ella an apologetic look as he wheeled

Phillip away. Ella watched him go, feeling strangely numb. She had waited all these years to see if he would notice her, care about her, love her?

I've been such a silly, childish fool.

Ella turned to stare out the window again, watching the light fade into evening. She had not moved once in several hours, and her body was stiff as she turned to leave the library. Inside she felt cold and numb, as though she'd spent the last few hours in the gardens without a coat.

"Ella?" Charles stood in the doorway. "Phillip has just left for his townhouse. Dr. Shreve thought it was safe enough for him to be moved. I thought you should know. He said to thank you for all that you've done."

Ella bit her lip as tears filled her eyes.

Do not cry. You must not let him see any tears.

Charles came deeper into the library. "Little bit?" She knew he would see through her if she tried to hide her pain.

"I'm fine, Charles. Truly."

Please go. Leave me to my broken heart.

"Ella..." The way he said her name, he knew without even seeing her face. Charles always knew her, as the oldest child always knows the youngest. It was a bond they'd shared since she was born.

She spun to look at him, her lips quivering as she desperately tried to hold herself together. "Charles."

"Yes?"

"Do you believe in love at first sight?"

Her brother joined her at the window in quiet contemplation.

He clasped his hands behind his back and watched the evening shadows upon the snow with her. "Love at first sight?"

"Yes. As though the person you saw that first time *belonged* to you, even before you knew their name." She expected her brother to tease her, to remind her that she was forever too young to fall in love and get married. But he didn't.

"I know the feeling exactly. You wonder how on earth you could even draw breath all the days before you set your eyes upon them. Because once you've seen them, everything else simply fades compared to their brilliance."

Ella's lips parted in stunned silence. He'd never spoken of love before, never kept a mistress for more than a few months. Yet now he was utterly changed. He seemed settled, grounded in a way he'd never been before.

"You speak of Lily Wycliff?" she asked.

"And you speak of Phillip?" he replied.

She gave his arm a tender squeeze and kissed his cheek before she left him to gaze upon the snow. "Perhaps one of us will have true happiness."

As she left the library, she glimpsed her book about Pompeii. She hadn't read it in five long years.

I know how their story ends; it is time I let go of the past.

5

One year later

"If I have to listen to one more man explain to me that business and politics are not things to concern myself with...," Ella growled over the rim of her teacup.

"It is most frustrating," her friend, Audrey St. Laurent, agreed. "I often say some men need a good whack to the head...or between their legs, depending on the man."

Ella snickered but then sighed as her mood deflated again.

"What's truly bothering you?" Audrey inquired.

Ella glanced about Audrey's morning room, seeking a distraction from her mortification, but they were alone. A fire crackled in the hearth, and sunlight glinted off the snow outside. It was a perfectly lovely day, which made her black mood all the worse.

"At one and twenty, it seems I'm now to attract the worst sort of men. I was at Lady Hearst's ball last evening, and every single man I danced with lectured me about how fortunate I was to even be dancing at my age. To make it worse, the younger ladies have taken offense at my being there. More than one lady said I shouldn't even be there because I am so clearly on the shelf. What shelf, I ask you? Are women like fruit? Do we turn sour after three seasons? I rather think I am better each year I get older."

Audrey's brown eyes glinted with amusement. "Fair point. I've often wondered what shelf it is society always refers to as well."

"Someone even said I was long in the tooth! What on earth suggests I've grown fangs?" Ella demanded hotly.

Her friend touched her arm. "Ella, breathe, my dear. Your face is turning an alarming shade of red."

Inhaling deeply, Ella relaxed as the burning sensation eased.

"You seem more upset than usual," Audrey said, her brows drawn together in worry.

Ella set her teacup down and looked toward the window. More and more often she had this wild compulsion to run out the nearest door and never come back. Something was missing in her life. Something she'd lost long ago, and she was afraid she would never find it again.

"Audrey, I thought I would fall in love again, that I

would feel that heat and light again, but I haven't. Not one time."

Last year she had confessed to Audrey how she felt about Philip because her friend had a way of understanding men and offering sound advice. But last Christmas had been a difficult time for all. Charles and his wife, Lily, had almost died when Hugo Waverly—half brother to Charles, Graham, and Ella—had tried to kill Charles.

It had been a vendetta long in the making, and even now Ella didn't know all the details. But all of Charles's friends, known as the League of Rogues, had been targeted by the man, including Audrey's husband, Jonathan. Ella's broken heart had been a small and inconsequential matter compared to that.

"You still love Lord Kent?" Audrey asked.

"I suppose I do, no matter how much I try to convince myself otherwise. I'm such a fool, aren't I?" Ella sniffed.

"Not at all. But *he* certainly is. Gillian, the Countess of Pembroke, said James told her that Kent barely leaves his estate. He's been a sour sort for the last year. James thinks it's because his leg still pains him. He still walks with a cane, I understand."

Ella brushed away her tears. She hadn't seen Philip since the day he'd left her in the library. Graham had gone to see him, but Ella hadn't dared to ask about him.

"I didn't know about his leg, or the cane," Ella whispered. Her heart ached with the thought that he must still be suffering.

"Yes, he's quite boorish about it, according to James." Audrey suddenly brightened. "Oh, I have a wonderful idea. Jonathan and I were planning to attend James's Christmas ball. He has invited you and Kent as well. What if we all went to Kent's estate and coaxed him into coming?"

"Oh, I don't know." Ella shook her head. "I don't think that's a good idea."

"Of course it's not good. It's *brilliant*." Audrey beamed and clapped her hands together. "Jonathan! I need you!" Audrey shouted.

Ella gasped as the doors opened and Jonathan St. Laurent, the younger brother to the Duke of Essex, came bursting into the morning room, fists raised.

"What's the matter?" he demanded, looking ready for a fight until he spied his wife, Audrey, standing there grinning at him. Audrey glanced at Ella and snickered.

"I love when he comes storming into a room to rescue me, bless him."

Jonathan relaxed and rolled his eyes. "One of these days, dearest...," he warned, but there was only love in his gaze.

"We are going to pay Lord Kent a visit on the way to James's party. See if we can't coax him to come with us."

"Oh?" Jonathan smiled. "Excellent idea. Good afternoon, Lady Ella." He bowed his head slightly as he saw her.

"Good day, Mr. St. Laurent," Ella replied. She envied the ease with which Audrey and her husband lived, false alarms aside. They were both openhearted and warm to one another. It was a special sort of magic to have a love like that, where there were no barriers, no distance, just a secret language built upon smiles and gazes burning of longing and fulfillment. She had thought she and Phillip might someday have that, each of them the night and the dawn, the sea and the shore, the spring rain and the blooming flower. Forever linked.

"Ella, say you will come. If anyone can shake him from his eternal melancholy, it's you." Audrey spoke the only words that could shake the walls Ella had built around her heart.

"Yes, I'll come." Loving someone who refused to love her back was perhaps the burden she was meant to bear, the struggle she was meant to survive. But knowing that did not make the weight of it any easier. Still, Audrey was right. He needed her right now.

"Wonderful." Audrey beamed at her, a mischievous smile upon her lips.

"But please, no matchmaking, Audrey. I must insist."

"Of course not." She circled her head with a finger. "See, my angelic halo is securely in place."

Ella shot Jonathan an amused look over Audrey's head.

Jonathan snorted. "It certainly is, securely resting on your adorable devil's horns."

"Oh!" Audrey chucked a tiny silk pillow from her settee at her husband, who caught it with a wicked grin.

"When do we leave?" Ella asked.

"Tomorrow morning."

"What? So soon?"

"Yes, of course. Christmas festivities wait for no woman," Audrey replied.

"Or man," Jonathan added, biting his lip to keep from laughing.

Audrey shot him an arch look. "I suppose. What is it you silly men do again? Oh yes, you drink too much and go outside to find a Yule log. I'm surprised no one's lost a limb to an ax yet."

Jonathan crossed his arms over his chest. "That, my darling, is a sacred rite, not to be mocked, even by beloved wives."

Ella was now the one who rolled her eyes. "I think I'll leave you two alone."

As she slipped past Jonathan into the hall, he whispered to her, "Never fear, I will endeavor to keep her from matchmaking."

"Thank you, Mr. St. Laurent." She laughed softly and closed the door.

A moment later she heard Audrey squeal and Jonathan laugh. Ella blushed as she collected her cloak and reticule and headed into the fierce cold outside. Her heart thumped wildly at the thought of seeing Philip again, but she was also afraid of how much it would hurt. And it would hurt deeply.

❄

THE FOLLOWING EVENING, THE ST. LAURENT COACH rolled to a stop in front of Lord Kent's estate. The grand manor house unfolded over four acres almost like a medieval castle. The south lawn was a great length of green grass that was currently embedded in heavy snow. The rows of gables and chimney stacks seem to pepper the roof with an indescribable gaiety that gave the manor house an air of courtly elegance. Swallows darted in and out of the tall, stately clock tower, chattering despite the cold winter.

"I always forget how lovely this house is," Audrey said.

"It is, isn't it?" Ella had never seen Phillip's country home before, and she couldn't resist taking in the magnificent sight. It was a lovely sprawling structure of stone and brick, with timber that must have first been laid as far back as the twelfth century. Yet she noticed clear signs that it had been remodeled recently to become the lovely pale-cream stone manor house that stood before her today.

"Go on, Ella. I shall be right behind you as soon as I find my gloves," Audrey said as she searched around for them.

Ella opened the coach door and stepped down with the help of the driver. She pulled the fur-lined hood of her cloak up around her face and approached the pair of open doors that led to the outer gatehouse. The door stood partially open, revealing a courtyard that led to a second gatehouse. It must have been a holdover from the structure's original design. She passed below the clock tower as she reached the second gatehouse. The sun was setting behind her, and the dark-gold rays illuminated the gray stone clockface with large brass hands pointing at the time.

"Hello?" Ella called out as she reached the door. It too was partially open, and she peeked into the entryway. She saw no one inside.

She tapped the lion's-head knocker hard against the wood several times until finally someone came to greet her. An older butler with dark hair graying out at the temples came down the side stairs.

"I'm so sorry to intrude," Ella said. "My name is Ella Humphrey. I'm a friend of Lord Kent's. I've come to fetch him for Lord Pembroke's Christmas ball. We have a carriage waiting for him. It's very comfortable, with footwarmers and a fine set of horses..." She stopped when she realized she was starting to ramble.

"I am his lordship's butler, Mr. Boucher." He spoke the name with a French inflection that sounded like *Booshay*. "I was not informed that he was to attend the ball."

"Well, he was invited. Would it be possible for me to see him?"

"His lordship is not quite in the mood for visitors." The butler was still frowning, and he flinched when a crash came from the upper floor. "Excuse me, I must see to that." Boucher rushed up the stairs to the left.

Ella stared after him. What was she to do? Leave? Yes, she should leave. She hadn't been invited. Yet something deep in her chest pulled her on an invisible thread up the stairs after Boucher. She chased after the butler, who ducked into a room. She skidded to a stop in the doorway and saw Phillip on the floor, one hand clutching his head and his other gripping a table for support as he tried to get to his knees. Boucher was beside him, trying to assist him.

Phillip's eyes locked with hers, and just like that, every feeling, good and bad, came roaring back.

"What are you doing here?" he demanded.

She still loved him, and in that moment as she witnessed him in pain again, she knew coming here was a mistake.

❧ 6 ❧

Phillip sat in the faded armchair in his study, staring into the crackling fire in the fireplace. His left leg ached, especially during the damp winter months. He rubbed his thigh, squeezing the muscles, and then farther down to his shin and calf. The muscles were still weak from the lack of use. But it hurt too much to walk, so he did so only when necessary.

A sound from the hall below caught his attention. Voices. *Who the devil could Boucher be talking to?* They'd reduced the staff over the last year, mainly because he had shut up most of the house since he remained close to his bedchamber and never entertained. He sat up a little in his chair, listening to the sounds of a woman. The pair of maids he still employed were likely on the first floor of the house at the farthest end where the other bedchambers were or in the kitchens.

"Boucher?" he called out, but his voice was hoarse

since he hadn't used it in what felt like days. He hadn't had occasion to see anyone or truly talk to anyone since last month when Graham had come to call. The memory still burdened him with shame. Graham had tried to talk him into returning to London, and they had quarreled about the matter. He'd said things he hadn't meant, and he had hurt his friend deeply. Graham hadn't returned since, and Phillip couldn't blame him.

The voices persisted, and curiosity drove him to reach for his cane. He steadied himself with one palm on the cane and set the other on the armrest of the chair. With effort, he pulled himself up and took a shaky, pained step. But the carpets beneath him had become rumpled, and he tripped. He cried out as he hit his head on the edge of a nearby table and a vase crashed to the ground.

Phillip lay on his stomach, trying to catch his breath. A wave of self-loathing rolled through him so strong that he nearly threw up.

Boucher came running into the room. "My lord?" The butler knelt beside him and gripped his elbow to help him up. The first time Phillip had fallen, he had tried to shove the man away, but now he allowed Boucher to aid him.

"My lord..." Boucher cleared his throat.

"Who were you talking to?"

"A young lady. I sent her away as you"

Footsteps in the doorway caused them both to look

up. Ella stood there, her blonde hair escaping from an ermine-lined hood. Blue-gray eyes filled with pity met his, and his world crumbled even further around him. He was a broken shell of a man on his knees before her.

"What are you doing here?" His question came out a rough growl, though not from anger but from disuse.

"I..." She continued to stare at him. "Lord Pembroke invited us both to his Christmas ball. Mr. St. Laurent and his wife, Audrey, were already attending, and we came here to see if you wished to travel with us." Her gloved hands buried themselves in her blue velvet gown as she watched him climb to his feet with his butler's help. Lord, the woman was a vision of loveliness, as always. Blue was a fetching color on her—it brought out her eyes and made her gold hair shine. It was as though she had fallen to the earth from some distant star and still glowed fresh with starlight.

Boucher handed him his cane, and he leaned heavily on it.

"I'm not going, so there is little reason for you to stay."

Ella's lips clamped shut, and her eyes became downcast as she slowly stepped back. It hurt to send her away, but he was a crippled fool. She deserved better.

Ella began to turn away but stopped and faced him again. "Do you truly despise me so much? Am I that pathetic in your eyes?" Her eyes were burning with fire and tears. The mixture of sorrow and fury made his body flush with heat and anger of his own.

"I don't despise you." What on earth had made her think that?

"I've done nothing but try to help you, and yet you push me away. I am done, Lord Kent. I shall leave you in peace, since that is what you seem to desire most." She didn't give him a chance to say another word.

"Ella, wait!" He hobbled after her, but she was too quick-footed. She rushed down the stairs and into the courtyard. He would never catch up with her. Still, he kept moving, slowly but surely, braving each step as he descended the stairs. Boucher followed him at a discreet distance.

He braced himself as he stepped out into the snowy courtyard and hobbled to the outer gatehouse, jerking to a halt beneath the stone archway. Ella stood a dozen feet away, alone. The tiny black dot of a moving coach far down the road held her attention. Two large valises sat on the snowy walkway beside her.

She'd been abandoned on his doorstep like a damned unwanted kitten.

Her shoulders were shaking, and a little muffled sob escaped her. He wanted to take her in his arms and murmur sweet things to her just so she would smile again, and to feel her burrow into him for comfort and warmth, even though he had no right to ask for such trust.

"Ella...," he whispered as he moved toward her, careful with his cane on the ice.

She turned to face him, her red-rimmed eyes wounding him further.

"They left me. I came back here to leave, but my cases were on the ground, and they were already going away. I called for them to stop, but..." She wiped her eyes furiously.

"Ella, please, stop crying." He must have sounded like a fool, but if she didn't stop, he wasn't sure what he would do. "You may stay here while we sort this out."

"Stay? Alone with you? I have no maid, no chaperone... Phillip, I'm ruined. The moment they pulled away, I was destroyed. Audrey must have intended this the moment she asked me to come here."

Phillip took careful steps as he came over to her, and feeling quite foolish still, he offered her a handkerchief.

"Dry your eyes and come inside. No one has to know you are here. I'm alone here with a small staff. No one will hear of this. I promise." He touched her shoulder and was relieved when she didn't pull away. He wanted to do so much more but dared not.

She sniffled. The tip of her adorable nose was red from crying and from the cold. "What are we going to do?" she asked as they walked back to the courtyard.

"We'll figure out something. I have a coach and a driver. I could arrange to take you to Pembroke's."

"How far away is his estate?" Ella asked. She kept pace with him, pausing as he stopped twice to catch his breath. It embarrassed him, but he couldn't go any farther without taking a moment to rest.

"In this weather? A little less than two days east."

"Two days?" Her voice was pitched high in panic as she gasped for breath. He caught her waist.

"Ella, breathe," he soothed as her face turned an alarming shade of red. He rubbed his hand on her hip, trying to calm her. Finally she seemed to regain control, and he reluctantly dropped his hand.

"Better?" he asked.

She nodded, and they returned to his home. The entry hall was dark and a bit dusty. Ella coughed, which made him wince. She couldn't stay here while his home was like this. He remembered how she had reactions to dust. Graham was always explaining how delicate she was.

"Boucher?" he called out.

"Yes, my lord?" His trusted butler was there, ready to help. The man had been his parents' butler, and he was one of the most faithful men Phillip had ever known.

"Please have the maids prepare a guest room for Lady Ella. One of the rooms past the gallery."

"The Lily Room?" Boucher suggested.

"Er...yes. That one." Phillip searched his butler's face for any hint of motive as to suggesting that room. It was directly next to his and had a connecting door hidden in the panels of the shared wall. A hundred years before, one of his ancestors had used it to meet his lover in secret. Boucher was well aware of that fact.

"And should one of our maids attend to Lady Ella for the duration?"

"Yes." Phillip glanced about the hall. "And perhaps we ought to hire back some of the staff as well." Boucher nodded in understanding. They could not have the Earl of Lonsdale's sister staying in a dusty, closed-up house. It wouldn't do.

"Ella, come sit in my study. The fire is lit, and you can warm up while your room is prepared." He gripped the banister with one hand and his cane with the other as he climbed. Ella did not rush up ahead of him; instead, she kept pace with him as they ascended.

"I've never seen your home," she said after a moment. "It's lovely."

"You're kind, but I have not taken care of it as I should in this last year."

She didn't correct him or offer any pitying comment, and for that he was grateful. When they reached his study, he hastened toward his chair but did not sit until she did. When she finally sat down, he sighed and almost collapsed in relief. He settled his cane beside him, resting it in the crook between his chair cushion and the armrest. When he looked up, Ella was watching him again, a disconcerted expression on her face. He could only imagine what she must be thinking. Was she wondering what his leg looked like now? Was he hobbling about on a shriveled limb?

"You've come so far," she whispered. "Your leg. You were terribly hurt, but you're walking very well."

Her words stunned him. He thought she would be disappointed or possibly disgusted. Yet she was praising him. As their eyes met, shock ran through him. He hadn't had the positive focus of a beautiful woman on him in over a year, and he'd forgotten how it felt.

"I am not walking as well as I had hoped," he finally replied, nodding at the cane.

"Oh, but the cane gives you a most distinguished look. At least, ladies must think so," she replied openly, honestly. She was so very much herself in that moment, the young woman he had met for the first time who played billiards and bargained for kisses. That was the Ella he had first cared about, the Ella he'd feared he had crushed with his harsh words. She was here. She wasn't broken.

"You think a cane is distinguished?" he asked, amused.

"Quite so," she answered without hesitation. "You are like one of Lord Byron's heroes."

He arched a brow at her. "Aren't they all rather tragic?"

"Well, yes, but only because he wrote them so. It doesn't mean a hero has to be tragic."

"Don't they?" he challenged. "A good hero must sacrifice something in order to be a hero. Doesn't that by nature make them tragic?" He was surprised by how much he was enjoying sparring with her verbally, and he wondered if she could refute that argument.

Ella's blue-gray eyes glinted with light. "Not at all.

How one views sacrifice determines whether or not it makes one tragic. A person can view the ability to sacrifice as a strength, a value that is worthy of praise and admiration. To me, a good hero takes pride in his or her ability to make noble sacrifices and not pity themselves for it."

He actually smiled. She'd outfoxed him on that point. "You are certainly right. I hadn't considered that."

Before either of them could say more, one of his maids entered carrying a tea tray. She set it down on the side table next to Phillip.

"Thank you, Cora," he said to the maid before she left. Then he looked to Ella. "Tea?"

"Yes, thank you. Shall I pour?"

He frowned. "My leg is crippled, not my hands. I'm quite able to pour tea."

Ella sighed in exasperation. "I did not ask out of pity. You know full well the lady is the one who usually performs the tea service, not the gentleman." She came over to the table and swatted his hands away. "If your desire is to be useful, add a few more logs to the fire. *I* will prepare the tea." He shot a glance at the fireplace. She was right—the logs were nearly ashes, and the room was starting to cool.

Cane in hand, he pulled himself to his feet. He was careful this time as he moved across the carpets and eased down in front of the fire. A wire basket held a stack of logs, and he used a poker to stir the flames back up to a hearty burn. Then he gripped the side of the fireplace and his cane to drag himself back up. The pain was still fresh, but after the long walk to the first gatehouse after Ella, he felt less stiff than expected. It was puzzling, but hopefully a good thing. He'd been so afraid to walk too much upon his leg. Every doctor who had consulted with him in the last year had insisted on further rest. Rest, rest, and more rest. He had been relieved at first, but now he was tired of it. Efforts that had come with ease before his injuries now taxed him greatly.

"Sugar?" Ella asked, calling his attention back to her.

"One lump," he replied as he returned to his chair and settled in. He accepted his teacup, and their fingers brushed briefly. Even in this innocent exchange, his body came to life at the small touch.

Ella removed her black velvet manteau and settled into her own seat with her tea. A long silence bloomed between them before she finally broke it.

"Were you planning on attending Pembroke's ball?"

"No, I was not."

"But you are friends with him, aren't you?"

"I... Yes. I am." He wasn't sure why he'd hesitated. He and Pembroke had been close, almost as close as he and Graham were. He had driven Graham away, and now he had pushed Pembroke to a distance. Just as he had so many others. Pain controlled him, had weakened him, and he hadn't fought it.

I am a coward, he thought. *A damned coward who doesn't deserve the friendships of these men.*

"Then you should come with me to the ball," Ella suggested, as though she had just announced it was a lovely day outside, not cold and wintry.

"No, I couldn't..."

"Why not? You are invited, you are friends with him, and I have no doubt that you are missed. It will be a lovely time."

"My leg pains me. It would be foolish to take on such a journey."

"Why?" she asked. Her eyes were wide, innocent, but for a second he saw a glimmer of something more cunning behind them.

"What do you mean *why*?" he snapped.

"I mean why would it be foolish? Yes, I understand your leg hurts, but that doesn't mean you cannot travel by coach in relative comfort to the ball."

She sipped her tea in such a ladylike manner, but he felt like she had called him out for his cowardice.

"Well... I..."

"Phillip, it would do you good to come. I know you do not like me or my company, and I promise to leave you to yourself during the journey. We can be two strangers traveling to the same destination." She sounded so polite, so calm and unaffected. But he had learned long ago how to read her face, the tightness to her smile and the pain in her eyes.

"Ella, we are not and never will be strangers. And never have I said I do not like you or your company."

Her eyes flashed with fire. "You have a fine way of showing that. You can't seem to leave a room fast enough when I enter it."

He growled a little. "That has nothing to do with not liking you. In fact, it's quite the opposite."

She stared at him, waiting for him to elaborate.

"Let me think on it. The ball is a few days away."

"You have until dawn," she countered.

"Then I'm not coming," Phillip replied almost petulantly.

"Coward." That one word hit him hard. He sucked in a violent breath, which made the old wounds in his chest pull tight. "You're frightened."

"I am *not*."

"Frightened of the ball, frightened of a few days in a coach with me, frightened, I suspect, of your own shadow."

He got to his feet and towered over her, growling her name in warning. "Ella."

She set her teacup aside on the table and stood up, their bodies only a few inches apart.

"Don't you need your cane?" she asked sweetly. Too sweetly. She was mocking him.

"Of course I do." He tried to move it, only to realize he wasn't holding his cane. He had taken several steps quickly across the room without it.

He moved his gaze from his empty hand to Ella's

face. She had a serene look of triumph in her eyes, and her full, kissable lips were curved in a smile.

Phillip backed away, stumbled more than anything, until he had his cane in his hand once again and a merciful distance was between him and the woman he wanted to both kiss and strangle.

"I think it's time you were shown to your room." He walked toward the door and called for Boucher. They waited for a minute outside in the corridor before Boucher appeared and led Ella away. Phillip couldn't take his eyes off her, feeling the distance and the darkness growing between them. Was she right? Was he hiding when he should be out in the world? He didn't want to think she was right, didn't want to think about how seeing her again, feeling her in his arms even for a brief moment, had sparked a light within the gloom inside his heart.

The sooner he could have Ella safely away from him the sooner he could go back to his life. His safe, quiet life here in his home, away from the world, away from pain.

A life of hiding like a coward.

Damn. Ella was right.

7

Ella followed Mr. Boucher through the house as he escorted her to her chambers for the night. Most of the furniture was covered in cloth to protect from sunlight and dust. Many of the tall paned windows throughout the house were shuttered, effectively sealing off the rooms from light and life. This beautiful house had been emptied of people. Closed off, just like its master.

They passed into one of the few more well-lit rooms, a long hall with paintings of fine-faced men and women. She glanced up at more than one of the portraits, seeing Phillip's eyes or chin, even his nose in several of the ancestors upon the walls.

"Mr. Boucher."

"Yes, Lady Ella?"

"Is he in much pain?" She was perhaps indelicate to

inquire about Phillip's injuries in such a way, but she needed answers.

Boucher paused to look at her in the moonlight. Whatever he seemed to be looking for he must have found.

"Yes. In the beginning, he couldn't walk. He lay in bed for several weeks, only moving with the aid of others or a Bath chair. For a previously healthy young man, being trapped in such a way was, I think, a greater punishment than the injuries. Once he started to try to walk, he fell so frequently that he became afraid to try, until he became as you see him now." The sorrow was evident in the butler's tone.

"I believe if he attends Lord Pembroke's ball, it might revive his interest in life, perhaps encourage him to try to walk more. Tonight, I admit I agitated him a bit, but he crossed the room perfectly without his cane." This revelation made Mr. Boucher's brows rise in surprise. "And the moment I called attention to it, he seemed to need it immediately."

The butler stroked his chin. "Ah... You believe he has come to rely on his cane too much. That it has become not only a physical crutch but one for his spirit as well?"

"Yes, that's it exactly."

Boucher eyed her sagely as they walked through the hall of portraits and entered a corridor with doors to a dozen other chambers. "I believe you are correct. What do you advise, then?"

"I profess I haven't the foggiest idea. But I wonder if it might not be good to open the house up again?"

Boucher answered with a nod.

"Then open the windows, let the furnishings breathe. Do it after we have left for the ball. That way once he has returned, hopefully in better spirits, he will find the joy of his home again as it sparkles and shines."

Boucher was smiling broadly. "We could decorate for Christmas. The master used to love Christmas. Perhaps we could even invite some of his closest friends over."

"What a splendid idea!" She was delighted to see how devoted Mr. Boucher was to his master.

The butler stopped and opened a door to his right. "This is the Lily Room, Lady Ella. I'll send Cora to you in a few minutes. Marcus, his lordship's valet, is also around to carry hot water for a bath, if you desire one. There's a section of kitchens just one floor below, so heating water is no trouble."

"Thank you, that would be lovely."

"I shall have Marcus start preparing your bath, then. Cora will bring you some dinner while you wait."

"Thank you, Mr. Boucher." She touched the butler's arm. "I'm glad to know Lord Kent has such devoted staff. He is worthy of it, even if he has fallen on hard times."

Mr. Boucher patted her arm. "I quite agree. His lordship is a fine man, and we are all honored to serve him."

When the butler left, Ella had a moment to explore

the bedchamber. Her bed was made of white birch. The wood had been delicately carved, including the four spindles, which glittered with light gold netting rather than heavy brocade fabrics. Lilies had been carved into the headboard in beautiful patterns, and the stems of the flowers had been painted green. Ella brushed her fingertips over them and was swept away in wistfulness. She'd always loved lilies.

The coverlet on the bed was icy blue and made her think of a lake covered with frost. The fabric was embroidered with thousands of swirling stars and more lilies. The stitching must have taken months, but the end design was exquisite. This room was fit for a fae princess. Not her, perhaps, but she had to admit she would enjoy sleeping here tonight.

A portrait of a lovely woman in the fashion of the previous decade hung above the mantel opposite the bed.

Phillip's mother? Most likely. She had kind eyes and an enigmatic smile that seemed to hint at old and happy secrets. It made Ella's heart break. She would have loved to have met the Countess of Kent. Her own mother had been friends with her and had spoken often of how sweet and witty she was.

There was a brief knock on the door to her bedchamber, and Ella called out for whoever was there to enter. The door swung open to allow Lord Kent's valet, Marcus, to enter, followed by a maid who brought tea. Marcus went into the dressing room to ready her a bath, and the maid, who introduced herself as Cora, set out a tray of cold cuts, hot stew, and some wine.

"Did his lordship return to his chambers all right?" Ella asked Marcus when he returned.

The valet exchanged a look with Cora before both of their gazes darted to the wall opposite her bed. "Er... Yes. Excuse me while I bring up the water, my lady." Marcus left, and Cora began to unpack her clothes for the night, laying out a gown for travel in the morning.

"I should like to leave early in the day. Would it be possible for the cook to prepare a basket for my journey?"

"Of course, my lady." Cora smiled warmly, her Irish accent sweet. "Should be no trouble at all. Mrs. Daley has many a fine basket for picnics. I'm sure one of them would do." She retrieved Ella's ivory hairbrush and undid her hair, combing out the tangles. After that, she pulled Ella's hair up into a loose topknot so it wouldn't get wet while Ella bathed.

Marcus filled up the copper tub and then left for the evening. Cora lingered in the dressing room while Ella bathed. Given the chill of the house and the weather outside, she didn't linger in the tub long enough for the water to get cold. Then, with the maid's help, she dressed in her nightgown and slipped her feet into warm green satin slippers lined with fur.

"I'll just turn the bed down for you, my lady." Cora pulled the bedclothes back and fluffed the pillows before she left. Marcus had loaded several logs into the fire, with extras to spare, and had used a bed warmer at the base of the bed to keep the sheets warm.

Ella sat in a chair by the fire, watching the flames burn for a long while before she contemplated going to bed. Part of her couldn't believe she was here in Phillip's home...alone and ruined. This was perhaps one of the worst Christmas holidays she'd had, aside from last year. Her dear friend, a woman she trusted, had just abandoned her on Kent's doorstep.

When I return to London, Audrey, you and I will have a talk about breaking your vow not to match-make your friends, she thought darkly.

Yet she couldn't stay mad at Audrey forever. Being here, despite the difficulty of the situation she'd been put in, and seeing Phillip, even know that this was a mistake, had filled the empty caverns of her heart again. She would give anything to have a life of laughter and passion with Phillip, the way Audrey had with Jonathan.

A thump accompanied by a curse behind the wall opposite her bed caught her attention. She hadn't imagined the sound, had she? She crept over on tiptoes and placed an ear on the wall, against a panel of wood painted to look like a forest. The wood creaked slightly and gave way a bit beneath the pressure of her leaning against it. *What on earth?*

She moved back from it to study the panel and then gasped. It was no panel, but a door. Ella moved her hand down the panel, seeking any groove or other sign of a latch. When she found it, she gave a little tug. The door pulled open on silent oiled hinges, revealing a short dark passage. Careful to leave the door open into her room, she entered the passageway. She felt like Persephone entering the dark realm of Hades when she encountered a door opposite her own.

It certainly was a passage, a secret one rather than a servants' corridor, connecting her room to someone else's. Another thump and curse from just beyond proved too much for her curiosity to bear. She pressed against the door, and it opened just as hers had. She peered around the edge and silently gasped.

Phillip stood in the center of the room, leaning on his cane. His chest was bare, and the muscles of his body gleamed in the lamplight. His body was beautiful, with lean ropes of muscles on his abdomen. She'd imagined seeing him again a thousand times, but she noticed he was thinner, much thinner than last year. He had lost much of his body mass due to being inactive. Yet he was still beautiful, still achingly, maddeningly handsome.

He stood there, offering his profile to her as he carefully lifted the cane off the floor and took a step without leaning on it. Then he cursed as he wobbled unsteadily. So that was what she had been hearing. He was attempting to walk without his cane. Pride swelled in Ella's chest. How very brave of him. She remembered how afraid she'd been to go into the gardens as a child. Doctors had told her she could catch a chill or a fever, or simply stop breathing due to the overpowering scents of the flowers and trees outside. But once she had gotten over her fears, she had learned she wasn't as fragile as all of the doctors believed. Now she loved gardens more than just about anything.

"I'm not a coward," he growled fiercely. "I'm *not*."

Ella realized he hadn't yet noticed her. He was talking to himself. Should she interrupt him or quietly fade back into the darkness?

Suddenly Phillip smiled, and the touch of humor about his mouth caused butterflies to lay siege to her belly.

"Little minx. She always did tempt me."

That did it.

"Minx, am I?" she said, torn between amusement and outrage.

He stumbled, dropped the cane, and clutched the back of the nearest chair to steady himself. "Christ! What is the meaning of this? You can't barge in on a man expecting privacy."

"These are connecting rooms." She pointed behind her toward the open door and passageway. "Might I ask what the meaning of *that* is?"

Phillip's face reddened a little. "I did not arrange to have you here for any wicked reason you would imagine." Phillip gripped the back of his chair and focused on her more clearly. The sweeping caress of his gaze was an almost tangible touch that made her shiver.

"You're undressed," he noted almost dumbly.

"As are you," Ella observed. Her heart was beating an erratic rhythm, and she flushed from head to toe.

"See? I was right." His voice roughened ever so slightly as he added, "Minx."

This time she wasn't mad. She simply laughed, and the frown that seemed to haunt his features vanished as he joined in.

"I don't suppose you have a billiard room?" she asked, stepping into his room.

"Not in this wing. It's on the far end of the house, too far for me to walk, but I do have chess." He nodded to a set laid out on the table by the fire.

"Could we play? I'm not up to reading tonight, and I can't seem to relax enough to fall asleep just yet."

"Are you implying my skills at chess will bore you into sleeping?" Phillip was teasing her, and Ella adored it more than she could say.

"Perhaps." She walked over to the chair opposite the one he held on to. His cane was lying out of reach. "Do you need it?" She nodded at the cane.

His gaze darted between her and his crutch. "No, not at the moment. Not if you are patient." He made a show of carefully coming around the back of the chair to ease down into it. Then he leaned forward and set the chess pieces to a fresh game.

"Boucher plays with me, sometimes Marcus," he added, flushing a little, as though embarrassed. It was essentially a confession that they were the only company he had.

"I would imagine Mr. Boucher plays a clever game of chess. Am I right?"

"You are," Phillip said with a chuckle. "Marcus is more of a billiards man."

"You still play, then?" she asked, leaning forward.

"No, not of late." He let her make the first move before he spoke again. "I closed up much of the house after... Well, the accident. It was much harder to move about between all the rooms."

Ella flinched at the word *accident*. They both knew that it had been no accident, no matter what the public at large had been told.

"I'm glad the man responsible is dead," Ella said, knowing she sounded cold and vicious. But she *was* glad. She would have killed that man herself had she been able to. Hugo Waverly had been the orchestrator of so many misfortunes among her family and friends. And the man Phillip had lost to at cards, Daniel Sheffield, had been Hugo's right-hand man in all of his horrible schemes. Yet Daniel still lived, and he'd even saved Charles from drowning in the frozen Thames. But even knowing that, she still hated that man for the pain he'd caused.

Phillip moved his piece, playing her in silence, but the silence was different than the last time they had been alone. When he'd left her in the library at Charles's house, heartbroken, that had been a stifling silence, a suffocating one.

"If I had listened to Graham, I never would've lost that last hand of cards," he said. "I almost got your brother killed that night. I don't know how you don't hate me." His eyes sought hers, and she trembled, pulling her shawl tighter around her shoulders.

"I could never hate you." Her mouth suddenly turned dry. *I could never hate you, because despite everything, I still love you,* she silently added.

They played long into the night, laughing about their mutual friends and stories from their youths. More than once their gazes met and held, and her body yearned for something more—and his did too, judging from the desire in his eyes. But they kept a distance, maintaining the pretense of a tenuous new friendship.

When she was finally exhausted, she rose and started toward the connecting door. Phillip reached out and caught her hand in his, and just like that, she was unable to deny how much she wanted him to kiss her... to do so much more with her. She stood still, her body humming, her mouth tongue-tied as he raised her hand to his lips and pressed a soft, meaningful kiss to the inside of her wrist against her rapidly beating pulse.

"Will you come with me to Lord Pembroke's estate tomorrow?" she asked, her words tumbling from her lips.

"If I come, it's on one condition," he replied, his voice almost as smooth as the wine she'd had with dinner.

"Name it and I will see it done," she promised. Whatever he demanded, she would make sure he had his wish.

"A kiss." His demand echoed her own from five years

ago. Her heart skidded to a stop. Elation and excitement rushed through her, only to be tempered by logic and reason.

"Why would you wish for that?" she asked, breathless.

"Because I owed one long ago to a friend and never paid it."

"It's a debt then? Nothing more?" Her heart hurt all over again.

He shook his head slowly as he stood, bracing one hand on the chair arm. "Because I wanted it then and never took it. Now...now I can't deny myself the kiss I should have taken then."

She swallowed hard. "What about the kiss the night of my debut? Was that not repayment?"

Phillip shook his head again. "That was a lesson. This is another kiss entirely. Allow me to show you the difference."

He beckoned her closer, and she came to him, drawn by a force that seemed written in the stars. He wound an arm around her waist and cupped her cheek with his other hand. Ella leaned into him, and his heady scent, like smoke and dark woods, lulled her under a hypnotic spell. She had dreamed of this moment, as foolish as that sounded, and now it was coming true.

Their eyes met and held as he gave her time to change her mind, but she answered him only by closing her eyes and waiting for him to kiss her.

"Part your lips, darling."

She did, and almost at once he took her. The kiss was hard, raw, and wickedly carnal. He thrust his tongue inside her mouth in a singularly erotic fashion that mimicked the play their bodies could have. Heat pooled between her thighs, and she whimpered and clutched his shoulders as her legs buckled. She was a breathless girl of fifteen all over again, yet this time, he was kissing her. And this kiss was the only one they might ever have. A tiny glow inside her burned with hope and bittersweet joy because she knew that she would at least have this memory of him. This was the Phillip he had been before his injuries had broken him.

Phillip's hand locked behind her spine, keeping her a willing captive to him. Her body tingled as he nibbled at her lips, biting them and licking away the sting before he kissed her all over again. It was almost punishing and angry, as if the years of frustration and desire held at bay were bursting free at last. All too soon he stopped. Their mouths parted, and they both panted softly, their breath mingling as he pressed his forehead to hers. Her lips burned in the aftermath, and she imagined his must as well. He licked his lips, his eyes half-closed. Kissing him with such reckless abandon had been intimate, yet now, holding each other in the aftermath seemed infinitely more so. His blue eyes, now a deep indigo in the lamplit bedchamber, swept over her face.

"You really should consider giving lessons in seduction. Ladies would pay for that." Her mind was still a bit fuzzy, and she felt both tired and a little giddy.

"There's only one person I would ever consider teaching." He kissed the tip of her nose and then let her go. She didn't move, didn't blink.

"So *teach* me. Teach me the ways of seduction."

Phillip's lust-filled gaze cleared a little. "What?"

"Teach me," she repeated. "I am twenty, Phillip. My marriage prospects are all but gone. I am on the proverbial shelf, or so I am told. I am tired, so tired of waiting for a man to notice me. I've decided it's up to me to find joy and pleasure. I want to find that with you, and I think... I hope...you feel the same. Won't you teach me what you know? We can be careful."

He stared at her for a long moment, so long she feared he would turn her down. "I'm not fit to teach you. I don't think—"

"You are," she insisted.

She realized she had pushed him too far tonight in her demands, so she instead kissed him with a delicate brush of her lips.

"Please think about it." She then left for the secret passage and returned to her bedchamber. She crawled into her bed and extinguished the lamp and lay down. Had she been too brazen making such a demand? Only tomorrow would tell.

❄

PHILLIP TOUCHED HIS LIPS WITH HIS FINGERTIPS. HE could still taste her, still feel her. Ella had challenged him in more ways than one tonight. She reminded him of the man he had once been. A man of passion and purpose. A man unbroken. Did she still see that man within him? He scraped a hand over his jaw, thinking. He leaned on the chair as he contemplated his choices.

He could stay here and let her go on alone to Pembroke's ball. If he did that, he'd fade into bleak despair forever.

Or...he could risk everything on one last chance of happiness by going with her.

He closed his eyes, relishing the kiss and the way she had looked up at him, as though he were a hero, a warrior come to save her—not that she needed saving. Though Ella was capable of taking care of herself, he wanted to charge in to her rescue anyway. She wanted him to seduce her, to compromise her—in secret, of course. Could he do that? Could he play the scoundrel?

It wasn't as though he was truly taking advantage of her, was it? She knew what she was asking; she knew the risks and consequences.

Phillip licked his lips, tasting her sweetness again, and made up his mind. He summoned Boucher and apologized for the lateness of the hour.

"Have my coach made ready at dawn. Have Marcus pack my valises for a week and the cook prepare a large basket of food for Lady Ella, Marcus, and myself."

"I assume you are going to Lord Pembroke's estate?" his butler inquired.

"You assume correctly." He waited to see if his

butler would bring up the fact that he and Ella were traveling without a chaperone.

But all Boucher said was "Should I send Cora as Lady Ella's maid?"

"Yes, yes, good thinking. Thank you, Boucher."

"Of course, my lord. I'll see it done."

"Thank you." Phillip bent to retrieve his cane from the floor and used it to walk over to the bed, but he found he only needed to use it a little.

His body was still wound up with excitement after kissing Ella. Kissing her the way he'd dreamed about for years. Perhaps it was that which powered him through. He set the cane against the side table by his bed, removed his trousers, and eased into his bed. He stared down at his leg, particularly at the spot where there were heavy scars on the shin, where the bone had broken through. His leg was not crooked, but it was weaker. He rubbed the muscles, gritting his teeth at the knot of pain, but he kept at it until he was too exhausted to keep going. He didn't want to fail Ella, and for the first time in a long while, he didn't want to fail himself either.

8

The following morning, Ella stepped out into the courtyard between the two gatehouses and blinked in surprise to find Phillip dressed and ready to leave. She'd thought perhaps after last night he wouldn't come. Yet there he was, eyes glinting with amusement at her astonishment.

He looked dashing in buff trousers and an indigo waistcoat. A greatcoat hung around his shoulders, only adding to the handsome picture he presented. Beyond him a large traveling coach stood ready. Marcus and Cora were helping the driver secure several valises to the back of the coach. The morning sky was still a watery gray as the sun failed to penetrate the heavy snow clouds that had gathered above them.

Phillip greeted her with a smile as she reached him. "Good morning."

She smiled back, but a sudden bout of nerves made

her tremble. Had she really asked him to tutor her in seduction last night? The reality of that moment was now a little daunting in the cold light of day.

"Come now, don't be shy," Phillip teased. "*That* is your first lesson." He offered her his free arm, and they joined the servants by the coach. "I had Marcus and Cora fetch some novels from the library for us to read."

He helped her inside and climbed in after her, using his hands to brace himself until he sat across from her. She was careful not to offer assistance lest he view it as pity. During their talk the previous night, she'd sensed that pity was the last thing he wanted or needed. Phillip removed his black calf leather gloves and tucked them into the pocket of his coat as they waited for Marcus and Cora to join them.

Once the coach was pulling out of the drive, Marcus immediately fell asleep in one corner after a busy night of preparations. Cora pulled out a basket of food and provided everyone else a breakfast of fresh oranges, bread, and cheese.

"You have oranges?" It was rare to have such treasures.

"My gardeners keep a hothouse, and we have half a dozen orange trees inside. They manage to grow them year-round." Phillip smiled as he peeled one. Ella did the same, relishing the sweet fruit as she slipped a slice into her mouth.

Cora began to mend an item of clothing to pass the time, and soon Ella was lost in conversation with

Phillip. It was so easy to talk with him. When he was distracted from his injuries, he was quite amiable, much like he'd been five years ago.

He told her about times that he and Graham had gotten in trouble while they were studying at Eton, and she laughed so hard she had tears in her eyes. Then he pressed her for details about her youth.

"Honestly, there isn't much to tell, what with Charles and Graham watching over me. But..."

"But?" Phillip pressed.

"Now I'm involved with a group of ladies who help one another pursue their passions."

"Passions? Consider me intrigued."

"Well," Ella said as she leaned in closer to whisper, "it's called the Society of Rebellious Ladies."

"I do love a good rebellious lady." Phillip's wolfish smile was also strangely tender at the same time. It was roguishly charming.

"And we certainly are that. Do you know Lysandra Russell?"

"The Marquess of Rochester's younger sister? Yes, she's rather charmingly eccentric."

"She's a dear friend of mine. The Society of Rebellious Ladies has been aiding her in sneaking into meetings for the new Astronomical Society of London which was founded last year. She's hoping to discover a comet, you see."

"Fascinating. How on earth do you sneak her into those meetings?"

"Lysa's so clever, but the men in the society don't wish to publish her findings. So we've done all we can to help her establish herself under a masculine pseudonym. So far we've had excellent luck. She's had two papers published in the last four months, and she's been able to attend the meetings...dressed as a man, thanks to Audrey St. Laurent's talent for disguises, of course."

"Of course." Phillip started laughing. "Lord, your society sounds like a formidable lot."

"Threatened?" Ella teased and gently prodded his leg with the toe of one of her boots.

"Not at all. Admiring is what I am. My mother was interested in astronomy. My father always wished she could have studied it alongside gentlemen who shared her passion. She would have loved to hear that a society to study it has been formed."

Ella tilted her head. "Your mother sounds like an amazing woman. I wish I could have met her."

"She would have liked you."

They continued to talk most of the day. The coach stopped a few times for them to see to their needs and have a quick meal and see to the horses before they continued. As the light vanished from outside and evening set in, the coach suddenly rolled to a stop, and Phillip sat up, puzzled. He opened the coach door. A heavy cloud of snow swirled inside, making everyone gasp and laugh. Marcus jolted awake, cursing at the cold before he realized he'd cursed in front of ladies and made a hasty apology.

"Everything all right, Henry?" he called to the driver.

"The snow is falling heavier, m'lord. We may need to stop early, leastways so I know where we are if it keeps snowing."

"What's the next town?" Phillip asked.

"Should be Aylesford, m'lord."

"Do you believe we can make it?"

"I believe so," Henry called down.

"Carry on as best you can." Phillip closed the coach door, letting in a second small snowstorm that made Ella laugh and Cora gasp and cover her mending. Phillip merely chuckled.

"Phillip, what if we become trapped?" The skies were darkening, and she feared for them all if the snow became too deep.

"Don't worry. Henry has been driving my coach for years, and he's a smart man. He'll get us to Aylesford."

Ella tried to distract herself with small talk. "I've never been there. Is it very pretty?"

"Yes, I think it is. 'Tis an old town." Phillip played with his cane, brushing his thumb over the silver knob. "It's an old Norman village with a church tower built into a steep walled bank along a river. Once we get closer, you will see the jumbled rooftops of the town staggered down the hillside where a large, regal bridge spans the river Medway." A smile curved his lips. "I took Graham fishing on the Medway once, when we were just leaving university. Not a bad spot to catch fish in the summer."

"It sounds lovely."

"It is. The bridge is old too. Legend has it the Romans and even the ancient Britons before them used it. Of course, the bridge itself is not *that* old, but where it stands, many men and women have used that spot to ford the river."

"That makes sense," Ella said, then yawned. It never ceased to amaze her that one could become tired from riding in a coach all day.

"You should rest," Phillip suggested. There was a softness in his voice that made her feel oddly vulnerable.

"I can never sleep in coaches," she admitted.

"Nonsense. You've never done the thing properly. Marcus, switch places with Lady Ella." Marcus moved easily into her spot as she sat down next to Phillip. "Now, rest your head upon my shoulder. It makes for a better pillow than the side of the coach."

Ella hesitated a moment, then rested her head against his shoulder. She nuzzled the sleeve of his greatcoat as she sought the most comfortable position, and before she was aware of it, she drifted off to sleep.

She woke an hour or so later and found the coach had stopped.

"Ella, darling, I fear we must get out and walk. The coach is trapped in the snow. But we are nearly there."

Phillip cupped her cheek and stroked her skin with the tips of his gloved fingers.

"Oh..." She sat up, stretching, and then his words sank in. "We're trapped?"

"The snow continued to fall too fast. Henry got us to the bridge at Aylesford. It's a bit of a walk to the nearest inn. About half a mile. Will you manage?"

"Yes." She followed him out of the coach. It was dark now, and she was worried whether he would be able to make the distance with his leg.

"What about the horses?" She stared at the patient beasts as they huffed and pawed in the darkness.

"Don't be worrying about them, miss," Henry promised. "Once his lordship gets to the inn, he'll send a few men back to help me and Marcus."

"He's right," Phillip assured her. "It's important to get you and Cora to the inn and warmed up." He started forward, the lights of Aylesford flickering in the distant snowy gloom.

Cora and Ella followed on either side of him, and Ella watched Phillip's movements, afraid he might fall in the snow.

"In 455, warrior mercenaries fought Vortigern, king of the Britons, on these lands," Phillip explained as they walked.

"How do you know so much about this town?"

Phillip chuckled, the sound carrying in the snowy expanse around them. "My father believed that if a man held title over a land, he ought to be familiar with its history. He once said to me, 'Most of these people will never visit their king in London, and so you are their ruler. You have a responsibility to them, to guide them and know them in order to help them move forward in life.'"

"Your father sounds like he was a wise man," Ella replied solemnly as she imagined how much it must have hurt Phillip to lose a father like that.

"He was wise, and that wisdom came from living among his people. He took my mother and me on many travels throughout Kent so that I might love these people and towns as he did."

They reached the bridge, and Ella saw the river was flowing swiftly, with small chunks of ice amidst the dark waters. Beyond the bridge was the town; a row of timbered Tudor-era houses met with a row of more modern stone structures. Beyond that was the dark shadow of the Norman church's tower.

"We'll head to that first timbered house," Phillip said. "There at the end of the bridge. That's the Black Prince Inn."

The three of them navigated the snowy bridge and entered the boisterous common room, where Phillip walked over to the bar and spoke with the innkeeper. A moment later, he returned with several room keys jingling in his palm.

"The innkeeper is sending three groups from the stable to help Henry and Marcus with the coach." He paused as he looked at Ella, his nose still red from the cold. "There weren't enough rooms available for everyone, I'm afraid, so I told him we were married. It is a risk, given that I'm decently well known here, but I doubt anyone will speak of it since I've asked for discretion. We are to share a bedchamber. Henry and Marcus will have another room, and there's a third bedchamber for Cora. Our room has only one bed. If someone were to discuss what they've seen..." He looked away, then drew in a deep breath before he faced her again.

"Phillip, I am fine with such an arrangement. I know the risks of ruination, and since I'm considered an old maid at any rate, I don't suppose I should be overly bothered to find myself ruined." Ella's heart raced as she said it, but she meant it. *This*, being with him and not caring about society, was what she truly wanted. To know him as a man, to fully explore herself as a woman in carnal ways. She would not change her mind about it. Yes, she had been panicked when she'd been abandoned by Audrey at Phillip's front door, but now she was resolved in her course. She refused to regret anything wonderful that might come, and she would accept any consequences that developed after.

"I cannot believe we are doing this," he muttered. "If Graham or Charles ever found out..."

He didn't finish the thought, though she knew what he meant.

"They won't. You've rarely left your house in the last year, and I'm less well known than you. The odds of anyone believing we were both here *together* is unlikely."

He didn't seem entirely convinced of that as he led her upstairs. Cora took her key and left them alone to settle into her own room.

"I assure you, my staff will speak to no one of what happens between us."

Ella placed her hand on his arm. "I know, Phillip. I trust you."

He unlocked the door to their chamber and let her into the room.

It was a quaint room with a cozy bed, a fireplace, and a pair of chairs. A silk changing screen concealed a large copper tub. She blushed at the thought of disrobing with him so near to take a bath, let alone sharing a bed with him.

Ella turned to face him when the door closed. She was fully aware of how vulnerable she was with him now, how if he was a different sort of man she would be in danger. But she trusted him. This was the man who had kissed her forehead and broke her girlish heart, the man who had driven her away because he feared his own weakness. He was an honorable man, and she had finally managed to convince him to be a little less honorable with her.

"You don't have to share a room with me. Say the word and I'll sleep in the stables." She could tell he was partially teasing.

Ella giggled and shook her head. "No, it's fine. Truly. I much prefer you here...with me rather than in the stables." She unfastened her manteau and pushed her hood back before she removed the garment.

"You're certain?" he asked as he removed his gloves and laid them on the table. The movement called her attention to his hands. He had lovely, elegant long fingers, yet his palms were strong and muscular. Her mouth ran dry as she pictured those hands upon her body.

"I am. It's been years since my debut, and in all that time, I've remained alone." She wanted to tell him that she'd waited for him to come to her and claim her. But she didn't want him to know how lonely she had been, how much she had longed for him and him alone.

He crossed the room, his cane tapping softly on the floor as he approached her.

"You're so..." He paused, his eyes fixed on her lips as he reached up to touch her cheek.

"Yes?" Her mind filled with sweet songs of joy as his lips moved in a way that promised pleasure and passion. How could she feel so attuned to him, the way two violins harmonized to create a singularly beautiful melody?

"I don't understand it."

"Understand what?" she asked.

"How you're not married. The gentlemen of London are greater fools than I imagined. You're simply perfect." Phillip lowered his head to hers and kissed her.

She drank in the sweetness of his kiss, and her body

quaked at his words. A dozen emotions rolled through her, and she was blanketed with sonorous pleasure deep within as she tasted his happiness upon his lips. He smiled while kissing her, and she had the sudden urge to laugh with the bubbling happiness that grew within herself. This had been the right choice, to be with him and not think about the future or the lonely nights she faced ahead. She would grasp these golden moments while she had the chance.

❅

PHILLIP WAS DAMNED, BUT HE COULDN'T STOP WHAT he was doing. She was so tender, so full of warmth and youthful excitement. Her kiss made him feel like the man he'd once been long ago. Like the man who'd danced with her in that ballroom ages ago, feeling her spin and twirl back into his arms. How she'd looked up at him when he'd kissed her beneath that starry night sky, and he'd thought in that moment they could have held the entire world between them.

Now he was kissing her again, and it was different. She was not a young, teasing debutante. She was a woman now, one who'd learned disappointments and heartache and clung to happiness that much stronger whenever she found it. He wanted to make sure their time together now was everything she'd dreamed of.

Her eager response to the touch of his lips or the flick of his tongue against hers brought back a flood of excitement. He'd thought he was incapable of feeling like this again, but he'd been blissfully wrong. A sweet melody echoed about him, and he groaned, pulling her tightly to him.

"I hear music," Ella whispered.

"As do I." He nuzzled her cheek, his hands finding a home at the small of her back. He admired her shape, the sweep of her spine and the flare of her rounded bottom that fit perfectly in his hands. Christ, soon he would have her body all to himself to explore. The peaks and valleys of her skin would be his alone to taste in ways that would make her moan and squirm. And then, only then, he would show her what true passion was.

"Are we both hearing the same song?" she asked as she leaned into him, embracing him in a most tender way.

"Yes. Wait..." He drew back and glanced about. Music was indeed filling the air. "It must be from the common room."

"It sounds wonderful." Ella sighed dreamily. The look upon her face was filled with unadulterated joy.

Kisses could wait. "Why don't we go down for dinner and see about this music?"

She beamed up at him, and he felt like a hero. "Oh, that would be lovely."

Quietly, they returned downstairs. He ignored the twinge in his bad leg and was careful to use the wall to support himself. The melodies of the violin grew louder as they entered the common room. A group of travelers and townsfolk gathered around the tables, eating and drinking. Near the fireplace, a violinist was tapping his toe and fiddling a lively tune. Phillip slid an arm around Ella's waist as he led her to an open table. He caught the nearest barmaid's attention to order dinner.

Men and women were singing and clapping to the tune. Phillip leaned his cane against the table and clapped along with Ella. She slid closer to him on the bench of their table, and he took a moment to give her waist a little squeeze, making her grin. Another young couple joined them at the table. By the looks on their faces, they had been recently married.

"Mind if we join you?" the man asked Phillip.

"Not at all." He held out a hand. "Phillip Wilkes."

"Lord Kent? A pleasure!" The man's genuine, honest smile followed his hand as he shook Phillip's. "My name is Francis Warwick, and this is my wife Bridget. I am still getting used to that, aren't I, wife?" Warwick teased the young woman, who looked to be close to Ella's age. He smiled warmly at Phillip and Ella.

"It's lovely to meet you. How long have you been married?" Ella asked.

"Only since yesterday." Bridget blushed. "We were married at the church on the hill."

"How splendid. Congratulations to you both!"

"Thank you," Francis said. "And you?"

Ella glanced at Phillip, her face reddening, so he spoke for them.

"Married a week ago. Private ceremony. We haven't

told our families yet." He hoped the man would have the sense to keep quiet.

"Mum's the word, Kent. I quite understand," Warwick said. "'Twill be a pleasant Christmas surprise, eh?"

"Indeed," Phillip replied. *Quite a surprise, if Ella's family were to find out,* he thought. "Are you traveling beyond Aylesford?" he asked Warwick.

"We were hoping to, but the innkeeper believes the entire town may be snowed in tonight. I suppose we'll continue the honeymoon here, eh?" Warwick glanced at his wife, and she blushed and smiled with obvious delight.

Ella's face fell a little as she looked to Phillip. "Do you think we'll be trapped here for more than a few days? I was so looking forward to Lord Pembroke's ball."

"Perhaps the roads will clear by morning," Bridget added, seeming to sense Ella's disappointment.

"Cheer up," Warwick told Ella. "The town has a whole host of festivities planned, and Aylesford is rumored to have the best Christmas pudding in all of Kent."

"My father used to tell me that," Phillip said with a chuckle. "I've never had occasion to try it here before, though."

"Would you like to join in the dancing?" Bridget asked Ella. She pointed to a group of young women who had lined up by the violinist and were starting to dance.

They were lifting their skirts just above their ankles to show off the clever tapping patterns of their feet.

"Oh yes, that would be delightful."

Ella and Bridget rushed up to join the other young ladies. Phillip watched Ella with hungry eyes. The elegant coiffure that she had arranged came loose in places, and her golden curls bounced down around her face as she danced spiritedly. Her cheeks flushed a strawberry red, and she moved her feet faster than most of the others. Once the violinist realized others were stepping back to watch her, he changed his tempo to match her quick dancing. She began to spin in a circle, holding her skirts to midcalf, uncaring of any scandal this might cause given that most of the people in the tavern were pleasant country folk less likely to fuss. Her blue half boots tapped and pointed as she hopped an elegant pattern that reminded him a bit of a Scottish ceilidh dance.

Someone with a Scottish accent shouted, "Fetch a pair of swords!" and another pulled down two swords hanging from a wall and crossed them in an X-shape on the ground close to Ella. She hopped easily over them, her feet landing in the spaces between the blades as the violinist played a Scottish tune to match.

"A talented wife you have," Warwick praised.

Phillip couldn't take his eyes off Ella as she continued to spin and dance. "She certainly is." The common room broke into song to encourage her. In that moment she was utterly bewitching, a true fae princess who had slipped between worlds to cast a spell over him. To behold her was to love her.

He *loved* her. He wasn't sure when his affection for her had become romantic love. The realization should have given him such unfathomable joy, but instead it cut him deep. He couldn't act upon his love. He could not ask her to tie herself to a crippled man, nor could he risk losing Graham's friendship, assuming he hadn't already lost it. Phillip was too embittered with his own condition to find a way to restore that friendship, but he could not afford to damage it further by letting Graham find out that he had seduced Ella. Not even a marriage would save him then. These few days with her were all he had.

9

The night was full of magic. Ella couldn't stop smiling as she left the dancers and returned to the table with Bridget.

Warwick poured them wine from a bottle a barmaid delivered to them. "Well done, ladies, well done."

The wine was sweet on Ella's tongue and went straight to her head as she ate dinner. Phillip kept a hand on her waist, so deliciously scandalous, even though they were pretending to be married. She could have floated away without a care in the world.

"Well, it's getting late. I think we'll turn in," Phillip said at last. "It was a pleasure to meet you both."

Bridget smiled. "As it was for us, my lord."

Phillip collected his cane, and Ella slipped her arm in his as they headed for the stairs.

"You were stunning tonight," Phillip said as they climbed the steps together.

"Was I?" She couldn't resist preening a little. She rarely received compliments from men who weren't her brothers.

"You were most enchanting." Phillip leaned against the wall as he unlocked their door and allowed her to enter first. The second he closed the door, she halted as he gripped her hand and pulled her back against him.

"Shall we continue your lessons now?" he whispered in her ear.

"Now?" Her head was dizzy as he licked the shell of her ear, and every bone in her body seemed to melt.

"Now," he chuckled. "And I have an excellent idea for your first lesson." He guided her to the wall. "Face here and place your hands against the wall."

Ella raised her shaking hands to the wall, feeling the rough texture of the wood beams beneath her fingertips. Phillip stood behind her, and the heat of his body warmed hers.

"Stay still and feel," he instructed.

And then he began to *touch* her.

His palms settled on her shoulders and trailed slowly down her arms. Then his hands came back up and moved down her sides. She giggled as he discovered a ticklish spot. He laughed as he leaned in against her and nuzzled her neck. Sharp jolts of need shot down her spine and into her womb. He was barely even touching her, but the feathery caress of his lips against her skin made her shiver and twist with desperate longing.

She gasped, pushing her bottom back against him

instinctively. "Heavens...that spot right there!" She never wanted him to stop, but if he did...she would die.

"You like that?" he asked, kissing the spot and sucking on her skin. The pleasurable need only magnified until her knees were shaking.

"Oh yes." She nodded wildly, and he gently sank his teeth into the soft, tender spot. She almost screamed as her body yearned, stretching toward something she was a little afraid of.

Cool air caressed her legs as Phillip pulled her skirts up. His body caged hers against the wall, and he slid one hand between her thighs. She yelped as he touched her at the very core of her aching center. No man had ever...

"Phillip...what...? Oh Lord..." She moaned as he stroked a fingertip through her slit, playing with her while he kissed the sweet spot on her neck.

"Close your eyes," he whispered.

Ella shut her eyes and then rolled up on her tiptoes as he discovered her entrance and slid one finger inside her. That single finger felt so tight inside her, and she wondered how the rest of him would ever fit when they came to that part of her lessons.

"So hot," he whispered. "It makes me ache to be inside you." He pressed his hips tight to her bottom, and she felt his heat and arousal. She'd never encountered anything more powerful than feeling trapped by him and enraptured in such building pleasure.

"I want you inside me." She rocked forward, moving against his hand. She wanted to feel his finger move inside of her, and he was quick to oblige, but she still wanted more.

"Soon, but not tonight," he promised as he continued to penetrate her with his finger.

His other hand swept over her bodice, cupping her breasts and then moving down to join his other hand. He touched her mound and the tiny bud that was now almost *too* sensitive. He caressed it, teased it, and finally, when she was shaking, he pressed down on it in tandem with his thrusting finger, and the world around her simply winked out. For a second she was weightless, blinded by physical pleasure. In time, the world bled back into her vision, and her gasping breaths filled the air.

Phillip held her in his arms. He dropped her skirts before he cuddled against her as she trembled. She'd never felt like this before, as though her entire under-standing of the world and her body had come crashing down and then rose up again in the most beautiful, exquisite way possible. She could become addicted to feeling like this.

"My God," she said in a daze as she turned to face him.

"How do you feel?"

Ella bit her lip, assessing the languid sense of relax-ation that now stole through her.

"Weak...but wonderful." She knew she would feel embarrassed later, but she wrapped her arms around his chest and hugged him. When she closed her eyes, his arms came around her back and his head lightly settled atop hers. She wasn't sure how long they stood like that, their bodies pressed so close.

"Then I taught the lesson well." He smiled down at her, and she wanted to never leave that room again so long as she was with him.

Ella lifted her head, suddenly feeling very impish. "Is there a way for a woman to do what you did, but to a man?"

Phillip's eyes widened and then burned with desire. "There certainly is, but that's a lesson for another night."

"But we don't have enough nights. Perhaps we ought to double our sessions?" She batted her lashes up at him the way she'd seen Audrey do dozens of times to her husband. Would it work?

He hesitated as a blush covered his face, making him appear almost boyish. It was utterly charming. She reached for the placket of his trousers.

"My leg...," he began again lamely as she started to unfasten his pants.

"Your leg is fine, my lord," she promised him when he looked at her. She needed him to understand that more than anything else. His leg would not frighten her away. He was a good man, and he deserved compassion as well as passion.

"Tell me what to do," she encouraged. Her body flushed as she unfastened his pants; they hung slightly loose on his lean hips.

"There are a few ways..." Phillip cleared his throat. "I could lie back on the bed or..."

"Or?" Ella gazed up at him, fascinated and aroused at whatever made him hesitate.

"Or you could be on your knees, but that isn't something a lady should..."

She placed a finger on his lips. "A lady may do whatever she likes in the bedroom. If I have learned nothing else from my happily married friends, it's that passion can and should be equal between men and women."

His eyes darkened to the color of summer storm clouds as she lowered to her knees. Then she opened his trousers, and he groaned as she put her hands on his hard length. She had to admit she was curious to touch him here, to see up close what she'd only glimpsed afar on marble statues, and never in this erect state. Phillip threw back his head as she curled her fingers around him and slid her hand up and down him. He rocked slightly into her touch.

"What should I do next?" She paused until she knew she had his attention, and then she added, "Master." She rather liked the idea that she was a pupil learning from a master seducer. It gave her the freedom to play back, to be a free, wanton woman who finally had the chance to embrace her own desires.

"Christ," he hissed, almost begging. "Do whatever you want, put your mouth on it or stroke it. It all feels good."

Ella ran her fingertips over the head and then down

to the base before she rubbed him several times in concert with his rocking hips, but she was more interested in what he meant by using her mouth.

"Do I lick you? Or take you inside my mouth?" She'd heard whispers of this but honestly had no specific information as to how to go about it. The last thing she wanted was to do it incorrectly and ruin the moment between them.

"Either, but inside your mouth is better." Phillip leaned back against the bed, clutching one of the posts for support. His bad leg trembled a little.

"Are you in pain?" she asked. "Your leg, I mean?"

"What?" He looked down at her, clearly startled. "No, not at all."

She saw the truth in his eyes. He wasn't in pain, so she focused back on their pleasure. She leaned in and licked the tip of his shaft, and the curse he muttered made her giggle. She liked having his full attention on her, knowing she was about to return the pleasure he had given her.

"Bloody hell, Ella. You're killing me." Phillip's eyes were closed now, and there was a look of sweet agony on his face.

She parted her lips and took him inside, trying to suck on him lightly, still unsure of the technique involved. He put one hand in her hair, coiling his fingers in the strands. She felt more connected to him now than she ever had anyone else in her life. Giving themselves to each other this way was intimate in a way she'd never imagined.

"You can suck harder if you want," he whispered hoarsely.

She obeyed and took him deeper into her mouth and sucked harder. He moved his hips back and forth, thrusting into her mouth and murmuring words of praise and delight. He suddenly stiffened and cried out, his body going rigid. Then she tasted him on her tongue. It was a salty flavor that she found she didn't mind at all. He sagged back against the side of the bed, now trembling. She rose to her feet and was shocked when he pulled her close and kissed her hard, possessively. His tongue thrust hard and hungry into her, and she melted into him, surrendering herself completely.

"How was *that* lesson?" she asked between kisses.

He tangled his fingers through her loose hair and gave a playful tug. Her hair seemed to fascinate him, and she liked that, knowing there were parts of her that he wanted to touch over and over. She wound an arm around his neck and buried her face against his shoulder, taking in his scent, branding it upon her soul.

"I think you passed that lesson, darling. Not that I would mind a repeat, of course." His smile was an almost silly grin as he stared at her.

"Why don't we get into bed and rest?" she suggested. His bad leg was still shaking, and she had a suspicion he was masking his pain now, at least a little.

"Let me help you undress," he offered with a wolfish expression that made her skin flush with fresh heat.

Ella offered her back to him as he unfastened the row of buttons down her back, then untied the laces of her stays. Phillip let each layer of clothing drop to the ground in pools of color. Then she was down to only her stockings and chemise.

"Your turn," she insisted.

There was something thrilling about undressing him and being so bare herself as she slipped the buttons of his waistcoat through the slits and then lifted the shirt over his head. His chest was as exquisite as it had been that first night in his room at the manor house. His chest muscles were strong and the ropes of stomach muscles well defined over his abdomen. She smoothed her palms over his skin, and the base of her belly quivered with excitement. What would it be like to have this man's body completely focused on her, pinning her to the bed, or up against the wall, claiming her? She'd never been one for fantasies, but Phillip seemed to create them by the thousands whenever he was near.

"What are you thinking about?" he asked, his deep voice sending chills through her.

"About you... About how strong you are."

He stroked her cheek. "I'd never hurt you." His promise was so tender.

"I know, but I was thinking..." She paused, her entire body flushing.

"About?"

"About how it would feel to have you use that strength on me...in bed...and how I'd like that." Lord, she was as wicked as any man, wasn't she? For wanting such things and voicing them aloud to a man she wasn't even married to. Deep down, she was no different than her wicked brothers, it seemed.

Phillip raised her chin so their eyes met. She saw dark lust churning in his gaze. "I would like that too. More than you know, darling. But not tonight. You should have a slow seduction—it will make the pleasure of your surrender all the sweeter."

Ella trembled at his words and couldn't stop wanting him to change his mind, but he was right. They had covered quite a bit.

He continued to remove his clothes with her assistance and finally stood there wearing only his small-clothes and she in hers.

He nodded at her legs. "Your stockings?" Then he patted the bed. "Up here, darling."

She hopped onto the bed and lifted her chemise up to her knees. Her thighs quivered with anticipation, knowing that his hands would be close to her core once again. His fingers untied the blue silk ribbons that held her stockings up and then rolled them down her legs. He kissed each foot as he bared it, and her head spun a little as he rubbed them.

"After all that dancing, I believe your feet deserve a bit of love." He chuckled when she moaned in delighted agreement.

"That feels magnificent. Never stop."

Phillip leaned in to steal a slow, open-mouthed kiss before he returned to rubbing her feet.

"That reminds me, how did you learn to dance like that? It's certainly not the way most young ladies dance in London."

Ella gripped the wooden post tightly as she tried to focus on his question.

"My...dance tutor was...Scottish."

"Oh?" Phillip sounded genuinely interested, so she continued.

"His name was Arthur MacTavish. Mother and Charles insisted I be taught the proper dances—cotillions, quadrilles, and the like—but MacTavish added a few secret lessons. He was one of my favorite tutors."

Phillip moved his miracle-working hands up her calves, rubbing out small knots in her muscles. She hadn't danced like that in years.

"And what sort of dances did MacTavish teach you?"

"What you saw was the ceilidh. It's a type of Scottish country dancing." She giggled as he tickled the backs of her knees.

"And what about the swords? Is that part of it? I've never seen anyone do that before." He moved to sit beside her on the bed.

"That was the Gillie Callum, or Scottish sword dance. The man who put the swords down on the floor tonight had to be a Scot. He winked at me, so I believe he recognized my dancing."

"I can't imagine Charles or your mother allowing you to dance about with swords on the floor," Phillip teased. She laughed, leaning against his bare shoulder.

"No, certainly not. But MacTavish said I was quick-footed enough, and I wanted the challenge, so he taught me in secret. MacTavish said the sword dance was an old war dance in the ancient clan days of the Scots. They used to have Highland games where the clans would compete, and many battles were prevented by allowing the clansmen to show their strength, stamina, and abilities when doing the Scottish sword dance. Now ladies learn as a way to show off their light-footed strength."

"So no battles will ever be fought if we have you dance over swords. That's an excellent thing to know." He kissed her temple, and she shoved him playfully so he fell back on the bed. She leaned over him, covering his face with kisses, and he wrapped his arms around her shoulders, holding her. She exhaled against his lips as she flicked her tongue against his. After their kissing finally paused, she lay back on the bed, her legs still tangled with his. She ran a hand over his bad leg, wanting to explore him more now that he'd relaxed. But he jerked at her touch, every muscle in his body going rigid beneath her.

"Did that hurt?" She studied the scars on his shin.

"No... I don't know why I tense up. I suppose I'm so used to pain that I've come to expect it at every turn." His tone seemed filled with regret and frustration. Ella rubbed her cheek on his chest and kissed his skin gently, reassuring him before she sat up enough to more clearly examine his left leg.

It was not shriveled or damaged, except for the scars. The muscles were perhaps smaller than his right, but that was no doubt from uneven use. He favored his good leg, making it work harder.

"MacTavish used to have a doctor come and rub my legs the way you did tonight. I was so young and weak when I started my lessons. But by the end I was strong. Incredibly strong. Have you tried that? Someone rubbing your leg?"

Phillip shook his head. "The pain was so bad for so long, I would not let anyone near it. The doctors instead prescribed laudanum, but I was afraid to become too reliant on it, so I didn't use it very long."

Ella understood that and was proud of how he'd braved the pain rather than rely on medicine. But he was still hurt enough that he didn't trust anyone near his leg, and that too she understood. When an animal was wounded, it would shy away from any touch, fearing only pain would follow.

I want him to trust me and trust that I won't hurt him.

"Would you let me try?" She stroked her fingertips over his knee. "I would stop the moment it hurt."

He was quiet a long moment, the doubt it conveyed filling her heart with sorrow.

Finally, he blew out a breath as though trying to relax. "Very well."

She moved down his body and began to rub her palms over his thigh first, squeezing the tight muscles. "Tell me the moment it hurts."

He winced a few times but didn't ask her to stop. She tried to remember all the ways the doctor had rubbed her legs. The way he had used his thumbs to dig into spots around the inside and outside of her legs, around the knee and along the shin and calf. Phillip fisted his hands in the bedclothes but still remained quiet as she worked down toward his shin. She was careful at first to avoid the knot of scars, but after he relaxed, she rubbed tentatively along the ridge of his shinbone and then along the dark-pink ragged line of scars. He hissed suddenly.

"Sorry," he muttered. "It doesn't hurt, but it is tight."

"Relax into the touch. Scars can be made smaller with time if you rub them."

"Oh?" He seemed interested in that.

"Oh yes." She lifted her right arm and showed him a faint white line down the inside of her forearm. "I got this while playing outside. I climbed a tree, and when Charles found me, I was so afraid of how mad he would be at me for climbing so high that I fell. My nurse at the time showed me how to take a salve and rub it into the wound. She told me that even after it was a scar, to keep rubbing. She was right. The scar was thick and hard like yours for a time, but look at it now."

He held her hand as he ran his fingers over the faded line. Then he looked up at her.

"You are..." He shook his head.

"What?" She was half excited, half afraid to hear what he might say next.

"You are magnificent."

He cupped her face and brushed his thumbs over her lips.

"Stop trying to distract me." She kissed him back before ministering to his leg again. She worked on his scars for at least half an hour, and when she was finished, she glanced over her shoulder at him and her heart stilled.

He had drifted off to sleep. The hard lines of anxiety on his face had softened, and for once he looked restful. She pressed a kiss to his lips before she carefully moved his bedclothes out from under him and then blew out the lamps and curled up in bed beside him, pulling the coverlet over them. He moved, wrapping his arm around her and drawing her into his embrace. She nearly moaned in pure exhausted bliss. Perhaps he would let her heal not just his body but also his heart.

And maybe, just maybe he will heal mine.

❄

AUDREY ST. LAURENT'S COACH STOPPED IN FRONT OF the Pembroke estate. The hour was late, but a groom met their driver, and a pair of footmen appeared to assist her and Jonathan out of the coach and to collect their valises. The butler met them at the door.

"Welcome, Mr. St. Laurent and Mrs. St. Laurent."

Jonathan brushed snow off his shoulders before removing his greatcoat. "We apologize for the late arrival."

"Her ladyship is still awake in hopes of seeing you tonight. She's in the drawing room." The butler collected Jonathan's hat and coat and Audrey's cloak.

Audrey brightened at the thought of seeing Gillian once again. She had missed her best friend. Ever since her former lady's maid had married James Fordyce, the Earl of Pembroke, she had been keeping herself busy running the estate. It had been at least a month since Audrey had seen her. Far too long for best friends.

Audrey thanked the butler and rushed along to the drawing room. Gillian was reading a book by the fire and turned when she heard the door open.

"Thank heavens you've arrived. I was worried the snow might've kept you away." Gillian hastened to embrace her, and Audrey laughed.

"Would I let a little thing like snow stop me? Goodness, that's what husbands are for."

"What are husbands for?" Jonathan asked dubiously as he joined them in the room.

"Ouch!" She smacked his shoulder as he pinched her bottom from behind. "Husbands are for digging out coaches from the snow so their wives don't miss out on essential social occasions. Jonathan, you clearly need a reminder of your duties and responsibilities." She was unable to resist teasing him at times like this. It was, other than sharing his bed, one of her favorite pastimes.

"Ah... So that's my function, is it?" Jonathan's mischievous green eyes burned with lust. "Then I shall endeavor to remind you of *your* duties, wife."

"Goodness," Gillie muttered. "You two haven't changed a bit."

"I suppose we haven't," Audrey admitted. "Husband, should we grow old and grumpy to better fit the world's expectations?"

"Certainly not," Jonathan replied with adorable smugness. "I plan to stay randy as a buck when it comes to you, my love. Where is James?"

"Playing billiards with a few other gentlemen."

"Then I think I'll join them." Jonathan bowed and made his exit.

Now alone, Audrey grew serious. "Now, Gillie, we have a situation. I fear I need your help."

"Oh? And what is the scheme this time? The Society doesn't meet until next month when Emily and Godric return from their holiday in Inverness."

"Oh, it's not that." Audrey blushed. "It's just that...I did something rather reckless."

"You? Reckless?" Gillian widened her eyes in theatrical shock.

"Oh, hush. I truly need help. I convinced Ella Humphrey to come here with Jonathan and me in our coach."

"Oh, and where is she?" Gillie asked hopefully.

"Er... That's the problem. I may have taken her to Lord Kent's house and left her there."

"What? How do you accidentally leave someone behind?"

Biting her lip, Audrey waited for her friend's displeasure. "I fear it was no accident." It had seemed like such a brilliant idea at the time, but as she and Jonathan had come the rest of the way, she'd started to worry that her plans to bring Ella and Kent together might have gone a bit too far. Jonathan had certainly been startled when she'd instructed the coach driver to leave, and he'd tried to stop the driver until she'd insisted that he should trust her. Now she no longer trusted herself.

"Oh, Audrey. Why? You know how reclusive Kent is now. He might be very angry at having to deal with an unexpected guest."

"But he didn't used to be reclusive. Remember how much of a delightful scoundrel he was?"

"Scoundrel? I remember him being a gentleman." Gillian chuckled. "I believe that since you grew up raised by your brother, who is most certainly a rogue, and with all of the League of Rogues as unofficial brothers, you view most men through a roguish lens. I believe you may be mistaken as to your perceptions of Lord Kent, especially where ladies are concerned. But yes, I remember how he was before the accident. Charming, warm, and quite hospitable."

"Well," Audrey said, leaning in to whisper, even

though they were alone. It was always wise to whisper about great loves, if only for the drama. "Ella has loved Kent since she was fifteen. She nursed him back to health after the incident. I thought it would be good to bring them back together."

Gillian tapped her chin. "And you think it was wise to leave her there? What if he no longer has any affection for her? You could force them both into an unhappy union because of this."

"He *does* have an affection for her. I have it on good authority."

"What authority is that?" Gillie was always the one to challenge her sources, and rightly so, or else Audrey would be prone to making things up simply to get her way or to triumph in an argument. They often had penned the Lady Society columns in the *Quizzing Glass Gazette* together, and the scandalizing social articles had made them infamous, but their identities as the authors were still a closely guarded secret among their families.

"Charles," Audrey replied simply. She had spoken to him only a month ago about Kent and Ella. That was how she had learned he knew Kent had feelings for his sister and seemed to approve of a match if it ever came to be.

"Charles? Ella's brother? How has he not shot Kent already? He and Graham are both quite protective of her."

Audrey nodded. "Yes, quite protective of her toward men who cannot be trusted, but Charles knows Kent is a better gentleman than any of the rogues from the League. He also knows that Kent loves her. Apparently, Kent spoke about her while he was with fever during his recovery. Charles was there to hear him call her an angel. If anyone knows a damaged man in love, it's Charles. I believe the only person who would hesitate on the match is Kent himself."

"And Charles truly has no objection?" Gillian pressed.

"None at all. He knows Kent is a good man. I suspect he also feels responsible for Kent's injuries, since Kent was targeted by Hugo Waverly as a means to hurt Charles indirectly."

"Would it be wrong if I thanked God that that man is dead?" Gillian muttered darkly.

"I'm sure he would forgive you for it." Audrey still had nightmares about that man. His body had been recovered, but Waverly's actions had left fear in all of their hearts. Everyone she knew felt that somehow his legacy would live on and haunt them all in later days.

"So you left Ella on Kent's doorstep. What on earth do you expect him to do?"

"If all goes well, they should be arriving here together, happy and ready to consider marriage."

"And if they don't? The storm shows no signs of letting up." Gillian's tone was full of skepticism.

"Then we will have James and the others ride out to rescue them. It's unlikely they would take anything but the most direct route here."

"Aren't you worried about them being alone? Or that they could become trapped in the snow?" Gillian asked, looking torn between laughing and rolling her eyes.

"Worried? I'm positively *counting* on it."

Gillian laughed and shook her head. "Why don't you go on up to bed. I will have James send a search party if they don't arrive by tomorrow."

"Thank you, Gillie." Audrey hugged her dearest friend. Leave it to Gillian to still be the calm and sensible one between them. It was what made them such good friends. One should always have a best friend who balances out one's impulses, lest one goes too far in one's schemes.

"I miss having you around to curtail me. Jonathan lets me get away with far too much."

Gillian giggled. "Yes, well, running around after you was exhausting. It's nice to be here with James. I feel like I've retired while still a maiden."

Audrey laughed. "Husbands are lovely, aren't they?"

Husbands were lovely, and she needed for Ella to claim the man who so desperately loved her in return. She silently vowed as Lady Society that she would not rest until she managed that particular Christmas miracle.

10

Phillip woke before dawn, feeling more rested than he had in a long time. A beautiful woman lay beside him, and memories of how sweet the previous night had been made him want to burst into song like a lovestruck fool. He'd given her pleasure and she'd returned it, and it had been going so damned well until he'd fallen asleep. Yet his body didn't ache, and his leg didn't hurt as he was used to first thing in the morning. He moved slightly, expecting pain, but the usual stiffness in his thigh and lower calf and shin weren't there.

He stared down at Ella's scantily clad body lying beside him. Had she truly rubbed his body last night, or had it been a sweet dream? He'd gotten so used to that, dreaming she was there to heal everything with her love and sweetness, that he didn't quite trust the reality.

No, it hadn't been a dream. She had pleasured him

with her mouth and almost brought him to his knees. Then she'd shown tenderness in helping him with his leg. God, the woman was exquisite in everything she did, from dancing to kissing and showing incomparable tenderness. He moved his leg, bending it toward his chest before he extended it out straight again. The change was surprising. His heart light, he leaned over Ella and pressed a kiss to her temple. She sighed dreamily and murmured his name. In that moment, he felt whole in a way he hadn't in a long time. It scared him, because he knew how easy it would be to shrink back into his old patterns and embrace his old fears.

"Stay in bed, darling. I'm going downstairs for a bit."

"Must you?" Her eyes were closed, but she was pouting sweetly in disappointment. It made him remember how she'd used that mouth on him last night and how he'd decided in that moment she owned him. No other woman would ever make him feel like she had.

"Yes. And I promise to reward you when I return." He gave her hair a little tug, and the feel of the tendrils in his fingers was like golden silk. He wanted to bury his face in it as he made love to her, to feel lost in her all over.

"What if I desire my reward now?" She opened her eyes and looked up at him, her dark lashes fanning over the loveliest eyes he'd ever seen. The quiet but fierce passion in her voice echoed his own. She was a woman who gave herself over completely to another person, and when he was with a woman, he was much the same.

"I am becoming less and less able to deny you anything, it would seem." He rolled her onto her back beneath him, enjoying the softness of her body and the way he fit so easily in the cradle of her thighs.

She sighed dreamily as he kissed her soft and warm lips, which always felt like coming home. In the last year, he'd often daydreamed about the kiss they'd shared the night she'd debuted. How she'd felt in his lap, all warm and sweet as he'd shown her the proper way to kiss. He'd let his mind wander to all the ways he'd wished he could have taken more of her that night.

"Don't forget my reward," she reminded him in a playful whisper.

"No, we mustn't forget that." He nipped her bottom lip, and she half whimpered, half giggled as he playfully kissed and bit her neck.

Then he pulled the bedclothes back and shifted down the length of her body, parting her thighs more to accommodate his shoulders. Her eyes widened and her legs trembled as he pushed her chemise up to her waist. A thatch of dark-blonde curls covered her mound. He knelt between her parted legs and caressed her inner thighs with light brushes of his fingers.

"Last night I taught you that a man could use his hands. Now I'll show you how a man can use his mouth."

Phillip gave her no time to stop him. He bent his head and kissed the top of her mound, and she let out an adorable little yelp.

"Easy, darling, it won't hurt."

"I know. It's just...so wicked." She looked down at him, and he couldn't help but admire the view of her breasts outlined in her chemise, nipples hard beneath the thin cloth. He would enjoy tasting them soon.

"Lie back and close your eyes," he commanded when she tried to sit up.

"You order me about quite a bit," she countered.

"If I recall, I'm supposed to be tutoring you. You did call me *master* last night." He kissed the inside of one knee and then moved his lips back down to her mound.

Careful to hold her thighs apart, he licked her center and chuckled as she jerked but couldn't escape him. He eased his tongue inside, making her writhe and pant. Her body responded with heat and wetness, and the bud of her arousal peeked out from under its hood. Phillip fastened his lips around it, sucking on it gently at first, then harder as he heard her whimper. Then he sheathed his tongue inside her and boldly swiped up the length of her slit until she was begging frantically for him.

"Phillip... Oh God," she whimpered, her head thrashing. "Please, I want you. Don't make me wait another minute." Her sweet begging was too much for him. He moved up her body, caging her beneath him.

"If we do this, we cannot go back. You won't be untouched anymore."

She lifted her head, a puzzled look on her face.

"You've already *touched* me, Phillip. No one else ever will."

She couldn't promise that, but he saw in her eyes that she believed what she said. He was too much of a scoundrel when it came to Ella to deny himself taking her in this moment when he'd wanted her for so long and she was begging him to.

"Are you sore from last night?" he asked.

"No—now stop delaying." She wrapped her arms around his neck and curled her legs around his hips, pulling him closer, a determined look now on her face. He settled deeper between her thighs and slid his drawers down with one hand and gripped his cock. As he guided the head of it into her body, she tensed.

"Relax, Ella, *please*." He didn't want to hurt her, but he would if she was tense.

He kissed her, his tongue seeking entrance once more. He played with her, stealing kisses until she relaxed, and then he pushed in, penetrating her. She arched her hips, driving him deeper. He groaned at the tight feel of her sheath around him, drawing him in until he was seated fully inside. It felt like heaven.

He rocked in and out, listening to the sound of her gasps and sighs. He circled his hips, which created an almost panting hitch to her breathing. They didn't speak as they made love together, and the silence except for the sound of their breaths somehow became sacred. They used their bodies to talk to one another rather than their words. His lips feathered along her jaw, and her hand slid up and down his back, her touch both sweet and light. Then he found that spot deep within her that made her cry out each time he thrust at just the right angle. She dug her nails into his shoulders, and he pressed harder, over and over like a man possessed. He *was* possessed.

She was so slick and hot, her body gripping him, and each time he withdrew and drove back in, she arched her back and whispered his name like a fervent prayer. He felt like himself again, like a full man, not a crippled fool. His desperate hunger to feel alive and whole again was unleashed upon her, yet she wasn't frightened.

"Harder," she encouraged him, her eyes lit with passion.

The last vestiges of reason fled as he pounded into her. Only rough pleasure would save them now. He had wanted to slow down, but he couldn't stop. He captured her arms and pinned them onto the bed over her head as he took her. Her pupils were wide as she suddenly went limp beneath him, but Phillip wasn't done with her. He pulled out of her, still hard, almost to the point of pain.

"Phillip, you didn't"

He rolled her onto her stomach and pulled her chemise up to expose her backside. The globes of her bottom were pale and delectable. He kissed down her spine until he reached her arse and nipped her right cheek.

"Oh!" She jerked in the bed.

He retrieved a pillow and lifted her hips, placing it below them, then gave her a little smack before he braced his legs on either side of her thighs. He opened her cheeks and trailed his fingers down to her slick wet entrance. She moaned and tried to push back against his hand.

"This is a unique position." He sank into her wet channel from behind and nearly groaned in sheer hedonistic pleasure at the feel of her beneath him, welcoming him inside her again.

"Oh...God," Ella moaned, wriggling her backside. "That feels wonderful."

"Good." It was the last coherent thought he was able to get out before letting himself go. He gripped her waist and began to take her hard and fast, pistoning his hips forward and back. The sound of their bodies hitting each other was sinful and set fire to his blood all over again.

"I like this...don't stop," she gasped into her pillow, her hands clenching around the sheets.

He drove deeper into her, loving the way he could watch his cock move in and out of her and listen to her gasps and whimpers of pleasure. He thrust, stroked, thrust again, until her inner walls clamped down on him and she came with a squeal and sank into the bed beneath him.

This time he couldn't stop. He rammed into her until he was blinded with one of the most glorious climaxes of his life. He was undone by her tormenting sweetness and by claiming her in a way no other man had before him.

He collapsed against her, kissing her neck, her face, anything his mouth could reach as she laughed in response. The sound of her joy was a gift he would never be able to return to her. Her trust and her affection had restored him to the man he once was, even if only for a few moments. Careful not to crush her with his weight, he slid off her, pulling out of her body.

She reached for him, her hand clinging to his hip. "Oh, don't. I want you to stay."

"I'm not leaving," he promised and brushed her hair back from her face.

She blushed, lowering her lashes. "I meant inside me."

"God, woman. You're going to be the death of me," he replied. His body wanted back inside her, but he needed time before he could take her again.

"Is that bad?" She bit her lip and looked up at him.

"Quite the opposite. Next time, I'll stay inside you as long as you like." He kissed the tip of her nose.

"I cannot believe we're talking about this." She buried her face in his neck.

"Lovers should feel open to speak of such matters." He couldn't believe how good it felt to have her in his arms, to feel so wonderfully whole for the first time in a very long time.

He waited until he was sure she was asleep before he slipped out of bed, kissed the tip of her nose, and dressed. When he was at the door, he stopped. He realized he had moved about the last few minutes without his cane. He retrieved it, more out of habit than need, and went next door to see Marcus. His valet was awake and preparing a tray for breakfast.

"Ah, my lord." Marcus smiled. "I was just coming to see if you and the lady were hungry."

"Leave it for a few minutes. Come down with me. I want to check the streets."

Marcus joined him in the corridor, and they went downstairs. The inn's common room was empty now, save for a barmaid cleaning the tables.

"How are the roads this morning, miss?" Phillip asked.

"Full of snow. The carriages are able to move. Some of the men from the town are digging the streets to make easier passage." The girl glanced to Marcus and blushed. His valet bit back a grin when he saw Phillip watching. The moment the girl walked away, Marcus rubbed the back of his neck.

"I assume you had a lovely evening last night as well?" Phillip remarked with a chuckle.

"I might have." Marcus watched the sway of the maid's hips.

Phillip and Marcus stepped out of the inn's front door and surveyed the streets, which were covered with two feet of snow.

Marcus shivered beside him. "Did you have a good evening, my lord?"

Phillip looked at his servant in surprise. "Pardon?"

"I mean, you seemed content last night. Happy even," Marcus ventured carefully, but he kept his tone neutral. The man knew better than to bring a lady's involvement into question.

"I am," Phillip admitted. "I do not know how long such happiness will last, but I will enjoy it while I can. Let's go back inside. It's too bloody cold out here." Phillip wanted desperately to get back to Ella.

❅

ELLA AWOKE TO THE SMELL OF PORRIDGE, EGGS, AND ham. She moved languidly, stretching her limbs, feeling sore between her thighs and a slight dampness in the sheets. Her face flushed as she sat up in bed. Phillip was seated by the fire, reading a novel. A tray of food sat on the table beside him, untouched.

"You should eat."

He looked over his shoulder at her, his mouth quirking into a grin. "I was waiting for you. Come." He patted his lap, and the invitation was too much for her to resist. She slipped out of bed and joined him. He curled an arm around her waist as she eased down on his lap.

"How do you feel?" he asked, his eyes tender as he looked at her.

"A little sore," she admitted. "But wonderful too. I fear you've given me a taste for sin."

"Have I now?" His delighted chuckle pleased her so much that her heart hurt. She loved his laugh, his smile, everything. She wanted only happiness for him because he had suffered so much.

"Yes, most definitely. Where did you learn such a unique *position?*" She whispered the word, unable to hide her scandalized tone.

"A man learns a few things over the years. I know of quite a few others we may try." He rubbed his palm on her hip, and fresh heat flooded her thighs. "But we'll wait at least a few hours. I don't wish to hurt you."

She wanted to tell him she didn't care. This morning had been everything to her. The feel of him inside her, merging his body with hers, and the sensation of being one with him had been something she'd never imagined possible with any other person. She now understood why her married friends acted so silly with their husbands. It was easy to become addicted to feeling like this with a man.

"Is it always like that?" She wasn't sure Phillip felt the same way, but she wanted to ask, even if the answer might not be what she hoped for.

He cocked his head to one side. "Like what?"

She curled her arms around his neck. "Like there was no end or beginning to us. That in that moment we were more one being than two." She laughed at her own overly romantic thoughts. "It doesn't make sense, does it?"

"It does," he insisted. "And no, that doesn't always happen. In fact, it is quite rare."

"Have you ever experienced it with other ladies?" She didn't want to believe he had been with others, but she wasn't a fool. Only she had been a virgin this morning.

"I haven't. I have not been with a large number of women, but enough to know that what we shared this morning was special."

"So you felt it as well?"

"I did," he admitted. But the joy she'd expected to accompany such an admission wasn't there. She saw instead only sorrow. Apprehension dug its claws into her.

"You don't wish to feel this way, do you?" She slid off his lap and retrieved her shawl from behind the dressing screen. She wrapped the warm wool around her shoulders and tried to fight the chill creeping in from outside and also from within her own heart.

"It is a bit more complicated than that, Ella. I'm a broken man. Men like me do not have happy marriages or happy lives. I cannot be the man to fulfill your desires as a husband."

She turned to face him. "Because of your leg? I thought you knew that I find no issue with it."

He shook his head. "You don't understand. You don't have to live with the pain, Ella. It keeps me from living the life that once brought me joy. I find nothing beautiful, nothing valuable now in my existence."

"Nothing?" That one word wounded her like no other.

"Except you, of course," he amended. "But you do not want a life with me. Not as I am. You cannot imagine"

"*Stop!*" She spoke harshly, her own tone surprising her. "Please, stop. If you wish to drown in self-pity, that is entirely up to you. But do not presume to speak for me while doing it."

Phillip stood and retrieved his cane. "I think I should give you some time to collect yourself."

"That is the first sensible thing you've said." She turned her back on him.

She couldn't let him see how much he had hurt her. Their joyful lovemaking this morning had meant nothing to him? This morning she'd experienced the purest form of physical love for him, and he had even admitted that he shared the same feelings. But then he'd cast those feelings aside because he was afraid and selfish. Loving someone meant loving *all* of them, even the darkest parts, but Phillip could not love himself. If a person could not love himself, how could he love others?

The door closed, and only after a moment did she look to see if she was alone. Her throat was thick with sorrow. She swallowed painfully and moved behind the changing screen to wash her face and put on a fresh chemise. Her hands shook as she tried to think. She could not continue to travel with him to Lord

Pembroke's estate. He would not come to the ball—she was certain of that. He would find some excuse to turn back. She had one thing left to try. If he wanted her, wanted what lay between them, he would have to come after her. All this time, she had fought for her love for him. If he wanted her, he would have to do the same in return. Ella tried not to think about what it would mean if he didn't. She tensed when the door opened again.

"Lady Ella?" Cora's voice drifted into the room.

"Oh, Cora, good. I'm glad you're here. I need to dress. Then I need you to go down and ask the innkeeper where I might hire a coach, if the roads are passable."

"Yes, my lady." Cora came over to her valise and sorted through the gowns inside the case. "What about this one? The taffeta day dress?" She held up an orange taffeta gown with slightly puffed demi-gigot sleeves that tapered to close-fitted wrists. It was a more modern dress than she was used to wearing, but she liked having a gown now and then that set her apart from the other ladies.

It was a lovely gown with triangular Vandyke points on the cuffs and a full skirt. Blue silk Vandyke patterns overlaid the orange skirts on the hem. She loved that gown and had imagined wearing it in front of Phillip, imagining how his eyes might light up. The bright colors of the gown mocked the pale, colorless feeling inside her, but she merely nodded at the maid, who helped her dress. Cora combed her hair back in swift, sure strokes, but Ella asked her not to pull it up.

"Leave it down, except the top."

Cora pulled back the top half of her hair and secured it with a large blue silk bow. The rest of her hair fell in loose gold curls around her shoulders.

"Let me go inquire as to the coach." Cora left her alone, and Ella packed the remainder of her clothes while she awaited the maid's return.

"There was one coach left to let. It's forty pence to reach Lord Pembroke's estate. I've secured it for you."

Ella thanked the maid with a sad smile and lifted her valise and started for the door.

"My lady," Cora said, holding her in her tracks. "If I may speak?"

"Yes?"

"You made him happy, miss. I cannot speak to why you're leaving now, or why he isn't going with you, but you should know, you *changed* him." The maid's eyes grew a little bright.

"Thank you, Cora. I only wish I had been able to change him more. It's up to him now. If he wishes to have a good and happy life again and to be with me, he must fight for it. He must put aside his fears and his pain and come after me."

Cora was quiet a long moment. "I think you're very wise, my lady. I do hope he's worthy of you."

"I know he is, but the question is, does he?" She thanked the maid again and gave her a quick hug.

Ella walked downstairs and past Phillip, who sat at a table with Marcus.

"Ella? Wait, where are you going?" He followed her to the door of the inn.

"Phillip, we've had a wonderful time. I learned much from your lessons, and I am grateful for all that you've shown me. Truly. But it is best if I go on alone. I've hired a coach, and the roads are now passable."

"Ella..." He whispered her name brokenly, and the sound carved an abyss within her heart, filling it with unspeakable pain.

"Phillip, I have loved you with *all* that I am, with every breath in me since I was fifteen. I never stopped. But I must move on. I have to let go of that, of you. You don't want me. I never expected you to. *Hoped*, yes, but I'm not so silly now as I was at fifteen. You have chosen pain over joy. You are right. I cannot love a man who does that, and I deserve happiness, even if that means learning to live without you." She drew a deep, shuddering breath and blinked back tears.

Phillip reached up to cup her face, his blue eyes full of storm clouds. He didn't speak. He lowered his head, giving her time to pull away, but she couldn't resist one last taste of him, even as tears streamed down her cheeks. It was a featherlight kiss, containing the ghost of the passion they had shared hours ago. It was a kiss of goodbye, a kiss of regrets and bittersweet apologies. When they broke apart, she hoped he would say something to change her mind.

Fight for me, damn you. Realize that you have worth, Phillip.

"You deserve a hero, Ella. A man who can fight the world for you, a man who will never disappoint you with his failings. I pray you find him." His hoarse words only doubled the pain inside her chest.

"I found *you*. I never needed a hero. I only needed *you*, Phillip, failings and all. You know where to find me, if you choose to fight for what we have. I'll carry the hope in my heart that you love me enough to realize that you're the strongest man I know. You have nothing left to fear in life if you only choose to love." She brushed the hair out of his eyes one last time and then left for the waiting coach. The driver took her valise, and she climbed into the coach.

It took every bit of her will not to turn and look back. The coach rolled away from the quaint little inn, and she broke down as despair carried away the shattered pieces of her heart. She had but one glimmer of hope to cling to, that he would finally see himself as she saw him—a man of strength, a man worthy of love—and at long last, he would let go of his pain and choose happiness.

❧ 11 ❧

The roads proved to be quite passable as sunlight melted much of the last evening's snowfall. Ella leaned against the side of the coach, watching sunlight glint off the snow like diamonds scattered on the surface of a white sheet. The rocking rhythm of the coach and the thudding sounds of the hooves lulled her into a numb state somewhere between wakefulness and slumber. She tried not to let her mind drift back to this morning, but it seemed determined to replay flashes of their lovemaking.

The way Phillip's eyes lit up between slow kisses, how it felt to thread her fingers through his hair, the sighs he made as they embraced after coming apart. The way it felt to have his fingertips brush against her cheek. Even the way he spoke her name as she walked away. She would remember every little thing, the bursts of light and heat, and the cold sting of her breaking heart. Perhaps in time the memories would fade, but she doubted it. If only he was brave enough to come after her, to fight for her. Clinging to that hope was all she had left.

Ella placed a hand over her lower belly, wondering if life had been created in that moment of love between them. She hadn't thought of it, nor he, at the time. What would she tell her family if she was with child? They wouldn't force her into exile or disown her, she knew, but Charles and Graham would want to know who the father was. She wouldn't dare tell them. It would break Graham's heart. Charles might well challenge Phillip to a duel.

After everything that had happened in the last year, it wouldn't be fair, not to anyone. She would have to hold firm and not tell anyone about Phillip if she was indeed in the family way. There was a chance he would claim the child as his, but she would not make a demand of it. If he wished to continue living in his tortured world, she would not put a child through that. Her babe would know only love and happiness.

The thought of a new life inside her, the future fluttering of a butterfly within her, made her smile sadly. She would give this child all the love in her heart that Phillip had rejected.

By the time the coach arrived at Lord Pembroke's estate at midday, she had dried her eyes and painted a cheery smile upon her lips. She was shown into the grand home and was informed that the ladies were taking tea in the morning room. She let a footman carry her valise away and take her cloak before she walked into the morning room. It was full of women chatting excitedly. The clink of china cups and saucers accompanied the light gossip. But a hush fell in the room as the fifteen or so ladies noticed her.

"Ella! You've arrived safely!" Audrey leapt up and rushed over to embrace her and whispered, "Where's Lord Kent?"

"Not with me," Ella replied. "How could you abandon me like that?" she admonished Audrey in a harsh whisper.

"We didn't"

"You promised no matchmaking."

"I wasn't! You and Kent were already matched." Audrey's serious tone surprised Ella. "You only needed a bit of prodding."

Ella closed her eyes, trying to banish the hurt that Audrey's "prodding" had caused.

"What happened?" Audrey move them out into the corridor.

Ella bit her lip and fought off fresh tears. "I made a mistake, Audrey. I...Phillip and I...were together for a short time, and it was everything I had hoped. But he won't let go of his pain. I told him how much I love him and that if he loves me, it is his turn to fight for me. And I left him."

"Oh dear." Audrey put an arm around her shoulders, giving her a squeeze.

"What's the matter?" Graham stood not a dozen feet away, watching them with concern. She hadn't seen him in the hall.

Audrey hesitated to answer, and Ella wiped her eyes.

"It's nothing. I'm fine."

Graham's eyes narrowed as he joined them.

"Let me talk with her," Graham told Audrey. "Alone." There was no way to stop her brother when he chose to interfere.

"I'm fine, Audrey. I'll join you in a minute."

Once Audrey had left, Graham lifted her chin, searching her face.

"I know I've been a rather absent brother, even more so than Charles." He closed his eyes and sighed. "I regret that more than anything. Tell me, Ella. What's wrong? Let me help."

Ella gripped his wrist, squeezing it gently.

"My heart is broken. I'm not sure you could do much to fix it."

His face paled. "What? When?"

Ella chuckled, but the sound was so full of sorrow it almost turned into a sob.

"Who is it? Who didn't want you?" he demanded. "I'll call him out."

"No, you won't." She straightened her shoulders. "Because I stood up for myself and told the gentleman that if he loved me, he would come after me. I'm strong enough to live without him in my life. I've faced hardships before, and I can do so again."

Graham cupped her chin and stared down at her in understanding. "You certainly have. Mother always thinks you're fragile, but I've known differently for a long time."

"You have?" She raised her brows in surprise.

Her brother chuckled. "I saw you and MacTavish dancing with the swords on the floor one afternoon. I almost rushed in to stop you, but then I saw you dancing, the way your face lit up and how quick your feet moved and how MacTavish was clapping in delight. I realized then that you'd grown up on me somehow, and you didn't need an older brother's overprotective actions ruining your dance lesson because you were perfectly fine and healthy." He chucked her under the chin as though she were a child again.

"I doubt you'll ever surrender your need to protect me." She couldn't resist teasing him.

"Of course not, but I'm more than aware that you are your own woman in charge of your own destiny, and you're strong. Any man you love will have the good sense to come after you. If he doesn't, he doesn't deserve you."

Ella managed a smile. "On this we agree." But she secretly wished that Phillip would prove her heart right, that he was the man destined for her and worthy of her love.

"So, shall we sit somewhere and talk?"

"No, we're going to have a lovely Christmastime here with our friends, and you will dance with me

LAUREN SMITH

tonight. It's Christmas, after all, and I won't let anything ruin it."

Graham studied her a moment longer. "I'm proud of you, Ella."

Ella didn't miss the honesty in her brother's tone. "Thank you, Graham." She hugged him. "What do you say we go play billiards? I've gotten quite good at it, you know."

"Have you?" He laughed. "Billiards it is." He slipped her arm in his, and they headed toward the games room. She wanted new memories, happy ones to overshadow her heartbreak, and she knew Graham would not let her down, not this time.

❄

FROM THE MOMENT PHILLIP LET ELLA WALK AWAY, HE felt lost, more broken than he had ever been. It almost crippled him. He stumbled out into the snow, Marcus calling after him, but he didn't look back. He wandered into the woods, his thoughts slicing through his skull with pain. He stumbled and fell, his cane sinking deep into the snow. Rather than standing, he curled up, his hands resting on his knees, and wept like a child. He was blinded by pain, so much pain, and none of it was in his leg. It came from his heart.

It was Cora who finally found him. She stumbled into view, bundled up in a heavy woolen cloak. She knelt down by his side. She didn't speak; she simply curled her arms around him, holding him. This simple kindness from the maid calmed him, and he controlled his grief enough to speak.

"Why did I let her go?" he asked, his voice scraping against gravel in his throat. Ella had made everything feel possible in his life again, but he'd been so afraid to trust that feeling that instead he'd let her walk away.

"Because you love her," Cora replied. She let go of him. "But if you loved her more, you would go after her."

He shook his head, denying the idea. "I'm not...good enough for her. I'm broken."

Cora stared at him, no deference in her gaze. "My father lost his leg in Waterloo. When he returned home, he thought he was broken too. He couldn't walk without help. But my mother reminded him that pain is not weakness. Pain is the body's way of defying weakness. Every day you push harder because of it. Miss Humphrey understands that. She loves you. She sees no broken man, and neither do I."

"You truly believe that?" He was a little surprised by her candid honesty, but he was grateful for it all the same.

"I do. But you won't find her wallowing in the woods. Come on, up with you." She gripped one of his arms and helped him to his feet. Marcus met them back at the village, his visible anxiety lifting as soon as he saw them.

"You're right—I have to go after her and win her

back. Prove that I'm a man worthy of her love." He felt it now, that strength filling him again as he saw clearly what he needed and wanted to do more than anything else: find Ella and tell her all that lay in his heart.

"My lord, the men of the village requested you to help find the Yule log. I wasn't sure if we were to stay or...pursue the lady."

Beyond Marcus a group of a dozen men, presumably town leaders and businessmen, stood waiting and watching hopefully.

"You have time," Cora whispered before she stepped away and let him stand on his own. He kept a careful grip on the cane that Cora had retrieved and nodded.

"Very well, then. Gentlemen, show me the way."

He spent the next two hours in the woods on the hill by the old Norman church, watching the sun set beneath the Gothic structure before a suitable log was found. He spent the entire time on his feet, relying less on his cane that he'd expected, and he was damned proud of that fact. He hadn't moved this much in months, and he'd forgotten how good it felt.

"My lord?" The innkeeper offered Phillip an ax. Phillip curled his hands around the handle, feeling a fresh sense of power rise inside him. Fueled by hope for the first time in years, he swung the ax a dozen times until the tree was felled and the log was made.

The men of the village came behind him, the large Yule log in tow. The boisterous singing of the townsmen following him had a strange effect. It bolstered his spirits, reviving him from the broken shell he'd been only an hour before.

Now, as he led the villagers back to town, he was ready to go after Ella. Ready to show her that he could be the man she deserved if she gave him just one more chance.

"Marcus, have my coach ready," he commanded as he left the townsfolk to celebrate the season.

"Already taken care of, my lord." Marcus pointed to the waiting coach. "The traveling cases have all been packed, and we are ready to leave whenever you like."

Phillip clapped Marcus on the shoulder. "Thank you. You and Cora have proven to be friends to me today, if it's not too bold a claim for your employer to make."

His valet grinned. "Not at all, my lord."

Phillip, Marcus, and Cora boarded the coach and settled in for the two-hour ride to Pembroke's estate. Once at the gates, the horses had trouble pulling the coach through the heavy snow. With a growl, Phillip grabbed his cane and climbed out.

Marcus followed him. "My lord?"

"No, it's all right. Stay with Cora and the driver. I'll send for help when I reach the house." He was not going to be weak anymore. He would walk a hundred miles in the freezing darkness to reach Ella. The distant lights of James's home twinkled merrily, beckoning rather than mocking him. If he could but reach the house and Ella, he might win back what he'd lost by his foolish fears.

His bad leg cramped within a dozen feet of the door, but he refused to stop. He nearly fell once when his right trouser leg caught on something deep in the snow and the fabric tore. He marshaled his strength and limped forward, leaning on his cane for strength, until at last he could tap the knocker on the door. A footman answered and offered him a bright smile.

"Lord Kent! Welcome! His lordship will be delighted that you've arrived." The footman glanced behind him. "If I might ask, *how* did you arrive, my lord?"

"My coach," Phillip said, panting a little. "It's trapped by the gates in the snow."

"Oh! I'll send some men at once." The footman helped him inside and took his coat and hat. "They're dancing in the ballroom if you wish to go now, or you may go upstairs to settle in first."

"Thank you." He knew the way to the ballroom, having been friends with James for years, but as he reached the open doors and gripped the gilded handles, doubt crept back in. What if Ella had hardened her heart against him already? What if he was too late?

Laughter and cheerful music slipped through the doors, and Phillip prayed that life would grant him one last miracle for Christmas. Then he opened the doors.

Dancers whirled by in explosions of colorful gowns. From the door he searched the dancers in the crowd, looking for any trace of Ella. And there she was, wearing an orange taffeta gown with a bright-blue bow at the waist, which trailed down over her bottom and flared out as she spun. She was the most exquisite thing he had ever seen.

Graham held her in his arms, twirling her too much, which made her laugh as she almost hit another dancer. Phillip found himself grinning like a fool. The two people he loved most in this world—his best friend and Ella—were here and happy. He could only hope that what he was about to do next didn't ruin everything.

He walked carefully between the dancers, heading straight toward the pair. People slowed to a stop around him as he reached the center of the ballroom. Even the musicians ceased playing as they realized what was happening.

"Kent?" James and his wife, Gillian, were dancing nearby and paused to stare at him. "Is everything all right?"

Phillip's face reddened as he looked down at himself and saw how disheveled he looked. He cleared his throat and looked to James. "My apologies for the late arrival and my current condition. The snow was quite difficult."

James came to him and offered a hand. "We're glad you're here."

There was no pity coming from him, just the warmth of an old friend. He moved back to Ella and Graham. Surprise was still plain on her face, and he thought he saw a glimmer of pride in her eyes as though she approved of him coming. He hoped he was right in what he was seeing.

What do I have left to lose? She already walked away from me once.

So he did the one thing that no unmarried titled man should *ever* do.

He walked up to Ella, and before anyone could think to stop him, he swept her away from Graham and into his arms, kissing her soundly, perhaps too much so given the gasps around them. When their lips finally parted, he didn't immediately release her. She nuzzled his nose with hers, her eyes dreamy.

"What did you do that for?" she whispered so only he could hear.

"I wanted everyone here tonight to know you are mine. I'm here...fighting for you."

She hugged him a little tighter before she set a foot of space between them. Phillip then turned to Graham. His dearest friend had his arms crossed, a slight scowl on his lips.

"You know what this means, Kent," Graham growled low.

"That I marry her?" Kent asked, facing his friend, expecting wrath, but he was unafraid. Ella was his now, and he wouldn't let her down, wouldn't disappoint her ever again. Because he refused to contemplate one more second where she wasn't in his life and in his heart.

"You're damn right you will. Won't he, Charles?"

Charles joined Graham, but he wasn't scowling. A soft smile was on his lips, a smile that Phillip had seen on Ella's face a few times in the last few days. A quiet joy that grew slowly inside until one day it was so strong it eclipsed all other emotions, erasing pain, erasing grief, leaving only the purest love the heart and soul could know. Charles understood then what Ella had meant, and he approved.

"Welcome to the family, Kent," Charles replied and offered his hand. "You almost died once on my account —now's your chance to live...with her."

"Thank you, Lonsdale. That's exactly my intention." Then he looked to Ella. "Would you mind taking a turn with me outside the ballroom?"

He had to tell her what lay in his heart and apologize for how foolish he had been.

❄

ELLA'S HEART WAS GALLOPING, LEAVING HER DIZZY AS Phillip escorted her outside the ballroom. The man had just walked into the ballroom and kissed her in front of *everyone*. That couldn't be undone. And then he'd told her brothers he would marry her. The entire situation still had her head spinning, yet it was exactly what she'd wanted to happen.

"Ella." Phillip stopped when they were alone in the corridor. "I'm sorry."

"For what?" she asked.

"For being blind, for being afraid. For letting you walk away. You were right about me. Pain ruled me. It dictated my life and owned my soul. But these last two days you showed me that it was possible to let go of all that. I was a coward not to trust you. So here I am—failings and all. Let me love you, let me give you the world, and I promise to be worthy of you and the love you've given me."

Ella swayed slightly. Drawing in a deep breath—she'd forgotten to breathe—she looked up at her beautiful Earl of Kent and saw in his eyes the future they would have together. Sunny picnics in the gardens, passion at every turn, and someday tiny little hands grasping fingers as they celebrated bringing new lives into the world together. She saw no grief, no pain, only a joy and a hope that mirrored hers so brightly that it blinded her with light.

"Yes." She answered the question he hadn't quite asked. It didn't matter. What he'd said, that was all she'd ever wanted, every dream she'd had since she was fifteen. She curled her arms around his neck and brushed his lips with hers. "I don't need the world. I only need you."

Phillip's strong arms held her close, no hesitation in his touch, and she loved that more than she could ever say. To be loved and wanted without another thought, that was all she truly needed.

"I think you've compromised her enough for one night." The pair of them spun to find Graham standing in the ballroom doorway, his sarcasm tinged with humor.

"My apologies, Graham. This time it was for tradition's sake." He pointed above their heads to the kissing bough that some mischievous person had hung. Ella laughed, only now noticing it.

Graham rolled his eyes. "So this is what it will mean to have you as a brother-in-law? Kissing my sister at every turn? Christ, I'll need more than a bottle of brandy to survive family dinners." He turned to go back inside, but Ella heard him chuckling as he did so.

"I hope he isn't truly upset," Phillip mused.

"He isn't. He loves you, Phillip." She leaned into his embrace, pressing her cheek against his chest.

"I'm sorry it took me so long to get here. The Aylesford townsfolk asked me to help cut down and bring in their Yule log."

Ella dissolved into giggles.

"What?" he asked, not understanding her humor, but joining her in laughing nonetheless.

"I was complaining to Audrey earlier about the gentlemen and their Yule logs and...oh, never mind." She covered his face with adoring kisses.

For the first time since her father had died, Ella felt whole in body, heart, and soul. She pulled Phillip's head down for a kiss but couldn't resist teasing him. "You owe me a game of billiards."

"And if I need three lives? What shall I bargain for?" he asked as he cuddled her closer in his arms.

"I think a few dozen kisses will do."

She felt his lips curve in a smile against her own. "How about a lifetime of them?"

Ella lost herself in his eyes and nodded. "Agreed." A lifetime of kisses with him was a bargain.

Phillip kissed her one more time, a lingering breath shared between them before he spoke.

"I would like to dance with you, here, where I can go slow and practice the steps. It's been a while since I've tried."

Ella grinned. "Here is far better. I have my wicked earl all to myself."

Phillip set his cane against the wall, and with a few tentative steps, they began to dance.

EPILOGUE

Six months later

Phillip stood at the edge of the lake near his home, holding his cane in his hands. Graham stood beside him. They didn't speak for a long time, but rather listened to the wind rustling in the distant trees and the chatting birds. A fox cried out from somewhere in the forest. The summer sun warmed the water, and light sparkled off the lake's surface.

"Graham, I wanted to apologize again for that night we quarreled," Phillip said. "I said things that were untrue and unfair because I was trying to hide my own flaws." He rolled his cane in his palms, watching the light flash off the silver knob.

Graham nodded. "I know. But you weren't entirely false. I am a selfish bastard. Charles kept my family together, raising Ella and protecting our mother after our father died. I was a coward who ran away. I barely saw them. I didn't want to be around them and feel the hurt of losing my father all over again. It was better to bury myself in brandy and the pursuit of widows. I didn't even dance with Ella at her debut."

Phillip grinned. "I owe you for that. Best night of my life until last Christmas." Phillip hoped his friend would hear his sincerity.

"I'm sorry I didn't fight harder for you," Graham murmured. "That night in the tunnels. I saw you go down, and then everything just..." Graham's voice was hoarse. "I ran."

"You *saved* me," Phillip assured him and touched the other man's shoulder. "If you hadn't gotten out, Charles and Lennox would never have found me in time. I would have perished in the tunnels and would be haunting them to this day."

Graham chuckled dryly. "Lord, we are a pair, aren't we?" Another silence settled between them, this one gentler, less strained. "At least you are to be respectable now, what with you marrying my sister."

"I was *always* respectable," Phillip said.

"I know that you and Pembroke belong to that Wicked Earls' Club. You can't tell me that is an establishment of saints."

With a shake of his head, Phillip found himself grinning.

"No more wicked than Charles and his League of Rogues."

"Fair point," Graham said. "So, what did you bring me out here for?" He gestured to the lake.

"For this." Phillip held up the cane. "You told me once that I relied on it too much. You were right. Ella proved that when she came back into my life. I don't need it anymore." He wound back his arm and threw the cane into the lake. It sank out of sight.

"Phillip, that was a waste of a perfectly good cane." Graham chuckled.

With a groan, Phillip shot him a glare. "I was trying to make a bloody grand gesture."

"It was certainly grand. Wasn't the head pure silver?"

"Oh, bollocks. Maybe I should have someone go after it."

Graham was now laughing heartily. He slapped Phillip's back. "We should return. I suspect Ella will be looking for you by now."

They returned to the house, Phillip keeping up with Graham without the support of the cane. His limp, which had once caused such pain, was all but gone. For the last five months, he had been visiting a doctor weekly in London who worked his muscles and put him through a thrice weekly regimen of exercises where he strengthened his leg until it once again bore the weight of his body naturally. It had been difficult some days, but Ella had been there with him, rewarding him with kisses and driving him on whenever he wanted to give up. She was a miracle—his miracle. He owed her his life, his body, and most importantly, his heart.

Graham slapped Phillip's shoulder and smiled before he wandered off in the direction of the library.

"Ella?" Phillip called out for his wife from the main hall.

"Yes?" She came out of the morning room and smiled up at him. She looked radiant in a day dress of green silk, the embodiment of a beautiful summer day. He grasped her waist, holding her close so their foreheads touched.

"Up for a game of billiards, my love?" He gave her bottom a playful squeeze, and her breath hitched.

"Only if you agree to do that thing you did last time," she whispered.

"The thing where I make love to you on the table?"

A strawberry blush fell upon her cheeks. "Yes, *that* thing." Her fingers played with his cravat, and he smiled wickedly.

"We most certainly will do *that* thing." He threaded his fingers through hers as he led her to the billiard room. Being married to Ella made every day like Christmas, even in the midst of a lovely English summer day.

THANK YOU SO MUCH FOR READING *THE EARL OF KENT*! I hope you'll check out my book *The Last Wicked Rogue* where you'll discover the scandalous story of Lily, a woman who falls in love with Charles (Ella's older brother) while

pretending to be his valet! **START READING CHARLES'S BOOK HERE!**

FOR THE NEXT WICKED EARLS' CLUB STORY *THE Earl of Kinross* by Meara Platt turn the page for an exclusive first chapter preview or buy the book here!

Marcus Brayden, Earl of Kinross, never expects his Christmas gift to tumble at his feet, but it does in the shapely form of Lady Lara Le Brecque, his best friend's sister...

THE EARL OF KINROSS

BY MEARA PLATT

CHAPTER 1

LONDON, ENGLAND
  December 1814

"MOTHER IN HEAVEN," LARA LE BRECQUE MUTTERED, toppling over the high wall surrounding Marcus Brayden's townhouse and landing in an enormous snowdrift. It was shortly past dawn, although one would not know it by the gray clouds covering the sky that prevented most of the daylight from filtering down. She scrambled to her feet, her cloak and gown now dampened by the wet snow she'd fallen into, and hurried to hide behind one of the large holly trees planted near the townhouse.

Breaking into houses was not as easy as she'd first thought.

She was cold, wet, and winded, and hadn't thought to eat a bite before setting out on her clandestine mission. But she'd made it this far and was not about to turn back now. She tiptoed along the brick facade in search of an unlocked door or window through which she could crawl. Finding none, she began to climb up a frail lattice to the upper floor when two hands clamped on her waist and she was suddenly yanked down. "Ack!"

A big hand covered her mouth as she was hauled against what felt like a stone wall.

Oh, heavens!

Not a wall, but the muscled torso of a man who wore no shirt. "Let go of me," she mumbled against his hand, "or I shall report you to the authorities!"

Of course, what the big oaf who now held her captive must have heard was a muffled *"Mumph, harrumh, mumph, mumph."*

"Be quiet. You're coming with me."

She started swinging her fists, desperate to escape his clutches, but he was too agile for her and she hit nothing but air. Drat! He now had her pinned against his damp chest. Goodness, his skin felt warm against her cheek, and if she weren't so angry, she might have considered his clean, musk scent captivating.

"Stop squirming. You're only making it worse for

yourself," was all he said as he suddenly hauled her over his shoulder and strode inside.

He carried her into what appeared to be a study and plunked her down in a soft, leather chair. "Sit!"

As if he'd given her the choice!

He'd practically tossed her into the chair, although he'd been gentler about it than she probably deserved. She clasped the arms of the chair, realizing she must be in Marcus Brayden's finely appointed study. "I demand to see–"

Her eyes focused on this bare-chested man who was the size of a Roman gladiator and appeared just as fierce. *Marcus Brayden, Earl of Kinross.* Just the man she wished to see. "Good morning, Marcus."

He stood in front of her, looming so large, he filled the room with his presence. The fire roaring in the fireplace emitted a golden light, illuminating his features and enhancing his magnificence on this otherwise gloomy winter's day. *Oh...my...heavens.* She tried not to gawk at the dusting of dark hair across his tanned chest or the path that line of hair took downward to his navel.

"Bollocks, Lara," he said quietly, his voice deep and resonant as he rolled the "r" with the slightest hint of surprise. "What in blazes brings you here at this unholy hour?"

She had always been a little afraid of her brother's best friend, and to her dismay, still was. Simply put, Marcus was more Greek god than man. His body was hewn from granite. Massive, muscled arms. Sculpted thighs, not that she was looking...but she was looking, because he simply could not be ignored. He stood before her in the glow of firelight, and heaven help her, he was splendid.

His dark hair fell in perfect waves, framing his masculine face. His dark eyes were cold and assessing as he stared at her, awaiting an answer. A scar ran from the corner of his eye and down his cheek to his jaw, but that did not seem to stop the butterflies from their frenzied fluttering in her stomach.

He looked daunting and commanding.

Had coming here been a mistake? If she were an enemy facing this man, she would have tossed aside her weapons and run in the opposite direction as fast as her legs would carry her.

She cleared her throat and met his unreadable gaze with a casual air. "Is it early? Goodness, I took no notice of the time."

He leaned forward, his big hands suddenly covering her small ones that were still tightly clasping the arms of her chair. "How did you get over the wall?"

She gave a nervous laugh. "Funny story..." He had her trapped between his arms, but this was the least of her concerns. She was suddenly in panic, her composure in utter disarray while his hands touched hers.

Fireworks exploded in her body.

She knew her cheeks were on fire, for she'd felt the heat creep up them.

Marcus had always fascinated her. The way he commanded attention even when saying nothing, just folding his arms across his chest and listening to whoever happened to be speaking at the time. The way he moved with the graceful stealth of a lion. The aura of power that surrounded him. He'd held this mystique even when younger.

Indeed, he was born magnificent and was even more so now.

She took all of him in. Dark hair, dark eyes. Big, lethal body. "Are you going to put a shirt on?"

He ignored her. "It's barely seven o'clock in the morning, Lara."

"What are you doing without your shirt on?"

"None of your business." He glanced out the window to the sky which was overcast and threatening more snow. "I assume this is no social call. What are you doing running around London *on your own* at this hour? At any hour, for that matter? Does your father know you're here?"

She breathed a sigh of relief when he drew his hands away and took a step back. He'd been standing too close, almost nose to nose...and lips to lips, so that she could almost taste the coffee he'd been drinking only moments earlier.

She must have interrupted his breakfast, although she would have expected him to dress before coming downstairs.

She dragged her gaze from his mouth, knowing she

should not be thinking of how it might feel against her own. Or how nice and warm his skin would feel against her palms. "No, my father is unaware of my actions."

She tipped her chin up in defiance, but the gesture went unnoticed as her rogue stomach chose that moment to growl loudly.

The noise resembled hungry cats meowing.

He sighed. "Have you eaten?"

"I'm not hungry."

He arched an eyebrow. "Come with me. Do you like eggs and kippers? Don't think to play the coy miss and decline the offer. You've hardly got any meat on your bones. We'll discuss the folly of your presence in my townhouse at this early hour after you've eaten your fill."

She'd been a skinny, awkward girl the last time he'd seen her. She had filled out since then but was still on the slender side. Her worries were to blame for that. How could she eat a bite when her father, the Earl of Stratton, was under house arrest and her brother, Hugh, once the respected Viscount Brixham, was a hunted fugitive? He had somehow escaped his confinement in Portsmouth Prison where he'd awaited hanging for the crimes of piracy and murder.

The last she'd heard, he was sailing to the opposite end of the world to hunt down the man responsible for these heinous crimes.

As for herself, she was about to be put under the guardianship of some ogre cohort of the miserable judge who had condemned her brother. This man was determined to destroy every last Le Brecque, although she had no idea why. None of them knew this judge, Lord Alistair Dunning, or had ever met him before this nightmare began. "Will you kindly put on a shirt? And my visiting you isn't folly. Have you not heard what has happened to my family?"

"No, I've been home from France less than a month, and most of my time has been spent recovering from my injuries." Since she had yet to move from her chair, he did not force her up, but knelt beside her when he noticed she was trembling. "Lara, has something bad happened?"

"Very bad." But her eyes widened in concern for him. "You were injured?"

"Never mind about me. Tell me what's going on."

"Oh, Marcus. Where to start?" The upheaval concerning her father and brother had affected her in so many ways. Not that she cared for herself. Saving them was all that mattered. But she'd taken a few bruises along the way. She couldn't deny it hurt that the man she had been about to marry had begged out of their betrothal.

Too cowardly to face her, he'd merely sent a note to her father enumerating his reasons for ending their engagement in humiliating detail. His note went on to say that if her father intended to sue him, he could go right ahead. No court would ever rule in his favor, for he was a suspected traitor and his son was a convicted murderer.

Perhaps what hurt most was the lack of any mention of her. It was as though she no longer existed to Phillip, Earl of Wexley, this man she would have pledged to love, honor and obey.

Suddenly, it was all too much for Lara.

She buried her face in her hands and began to cry as she hadn't cried in all the time since the madness had begun. She'd had to be strong for her father and brother. She'd done her best to fight for them, but she'd been little more than a child when their problems had begun and was a mere girl of nineteen now.

No one had taken her seriously back then nor did they now.

Who would she turn to if Marcus refused to help? She trusted no one else.

He rose and drew her out of her chair to envelop her in the comfort of his arms. "Lara…"

Oh, heavens. She loved the way he spoke her name, could almost feel the deliciousness of his tongue caressing the letter "r". "I'm sorry. I'm so sorry, Marcus. I don't know what's come over me. I've never cried like this before."

"Which explains why it is all pouring out of you now. It's long overdue." His voice was surprisingly gentle, and his arms…oh, being in his arms was too wonderful for words. She rested her head against his chest and pressed her body lightly to his, suddenly needing to absorb his heat and strength.

After a moment, she withdrew her handkerchief to dab at her damp cheeks, but he eased it out of her hands and took over the chore. "Come with me. We'll get some food in you and you'll tell me all that's been going on. I'd heard rumors at my club the other day, but didn't give them credence. It all sounded too absurd."

"It's been a nightmare," she agreed, wishing her tears would stop flowing. But she'd opened the floodgate and could not seem to shut it.

"I should have called on you sooner, but the moment I was back on my feet, I was summoned to the Foreign Office, and it's been keeping me busy ever since."

She nodded. "There must be so much work to do to fix the damage caused by Napoleon and his ambitions."

"Yes, there is. Even though he is presently subdued, I don't believe this calm will last long. The French are restless. Now that I'm healed, I'll probably be called back into service any day."

As he raked a hand through his hair, she noticed a raw scar on the underside of his arm. "Marcus," she said in an agonized whisper.

He followed the direction of her gaze. "That? The result of a bayonet shoved through me...well, I don't suppose it matters."

"The scar on your face is new as well." She reached up to lightly trace her finger along his cheek.

He shrugged and gently nudged her hand away. "It is nothing, Lara, and did not prevent me from visiting your father sooner. I should have done so weeks ago." He tucked her arm in his and led her into his dining room.

Everything about this man spoke of wealth and power. His table easily seated forty guests. The crystal sconces lining the wallpapered walls shone like diamonds. A massive silver epergne, polished and gleaming, stood like a Roman guard upon the table. A large, mahogany buffet stretched along one of the side walls, and an enormous, floral patterned, oriental carpet of deep maroon, blue, and gold covered the floor.

"Impressive, isn't it?" he muttered, following her gaze as she noted every object. "They call that massive thing of polished silver on the center of the table an epergne, but it's just a fancy name for a candelabra. That's what I use it for."

Lara bridled at his remark. "I wasn't counting up the shillings in my head. Or calculating your marital desirability based upon it. Don't flatter yourself." Oh, blast! She was here to win him over, not insult him.

Fortunately, he did not take offense, the glint of amusement in his eyes quite telling. "Are you not the least bit impressed by my title or the wealth that comes with it?"

He'd been granted the earldom of Kinross by the Crown several years ago as reward for his war service. She'd always thought of him as Marcus, but now that he was Earl of Kinross, she supposed she ought to address him accordingly. "I am impressed, my lord."

He groaned. "You don't have to call me that. Marcus will do. I haven't been a wealthy earl all that long."

She managed a weak smile. "I'm very proud of you. Sorry I lashed out as I did just now. I'm not myself. In truth, I no longer know who I am amid this nightmare or who I'm supposed to be."

He flicked his wrist and a footman hurried over. "Some coffee for Lady Lara." But he rose himself and began to pile food on a plate. He set it down in front of her. "Start eating while I don some clothes. Don't run away or I'll come after you. We'll talk once you've finished. I've nothing pressing to do today. Even if I did, I'd drop it all. It seems your family is in dire need of my help."

She nodded. "Yes, we are."

Once Marcus left to dress, she picked up her fork and began to move the eggs around on her plate. She'd hardly taken a bite before he returned. He'd merely tossed on a shirt. No vest or cravat. Well, how did one dress for invaders climbing one's walls?

"Lara, you haven't touched your plate. Must I feed you myself?"

"No." She plunged her fork into a kipper and took a bite, then another. Finally, she set her fork down and began to talk while staring into those dead kippers and the lump of eggs surrounding them. "They watch me all the time, Marcus. They follow me everywhere. That's why I had to sneak out of the house early this morning. They think I'm still asleep. I'll have to sneak back home before they realize I'm not in my bedchamber. My maid will stall them as long as she can, but I dare not get her into trouble. She's my only reliable ally. If they dismiss her, I'll have no one on my side."

"Lara, who is *they*?"

She picked up her fork and began to poke at her pile of eggs. "I'm not sure. The villainous judge, Lord Alistair Dunning, for one. But he's just an odious tool. There's a larger conspiracy afoot. I don't know who's been bribing him. I have my suspicions, but I can't prove any of it. That's where I need your help. You can speak directly to the House of Lords. You can also get into the dockside taverns, into the back alleys and houses of ill repute to gain information."

"Or I can just threaten to break Dunning's neck if he refuses to tell me who's been bribing him."

She set down her fork again and smiled at him. "I like that plan."

He was seated at the head of the long table. She was seated to his left. He reached over and took her hand. "You do realize I am jesting." He ran his thumb gently over the top of her hand. "I cannot go around killing everyone who displeases me."

"I know." Her smile faded. "But I can, for I've fallen so low and am so very desperate. I will kill him. I mean it, Marcus. I won't hesitate to do it."

"Don't talk like that, Lara. We'll get to the truth."

"When? I don't wish to be clearing Hugh's name posthumously." She stopped herself from bursting into sobs again. "This judge is pure evil. I detest the way he looks at me. He's plotting to put me under his control next. I know this is what he intends. He'll appoint one of his toadies as my guardian. I shudder to think what he has in mind for me."

She was still struggling to hold back tears, but they trickled onto her cheeks anyway. What was Marcus thinking? He had to know she was held together by a thin thread that was about to snap. "I never thought myself capable of murder, but it turns out I am. I'll kill him if he touches me."

She expected Marcus to dismiss her remarks as hysterical, but he frowned thoughtfully. In typical Marcus fashion, he said nothing for the longest time. "Lara, do you truly believe he means to take guardianship of you?"

"I know it for a fact. He doesn't hide his lecherous thoughts from me. Of course, to the rest of the world, he's a pillar of the community. He claims some relation to the Duke of Wiltfordshire, that's how he's wormed himself into the highest circles. He sits on the High Court. I cannot be his only victim. He's done this to others, I'm sure. I don't mean taking advantage of young women, although I have no doubt he's done that. For the right price, he'll do anything to anyone, and won't feel a moment's remorse. He wasn't born into wealth despite his relation to Wiltfordshire, so I suspect he maintains his life of opulence by taking bribes."

"Tell me all you know about him. I'll ask around at the gaming hells." He released her hand with a reassuring squeeze. There was a lovely strength to his touch. Without it, she quickly felt bereft. "Sounds to me, he's a man with an expensive gambling habit. His clerks must know something of this."

Lara nodded. "He must give them a cut of his profits to keep them quiet. His bailiffs, too. I've managed to get no information out of them so far."

"They know who you are and that puts them on their guard. I'll have a Bow Street runner investigate. I know of a very good man, Homer Barrow. He'll get the truth out of them."

Lara took a bite of her eggs. "Thank you, Marcus. Oh, these are delicious."

He smiled. "Getting your appetite back?"

She nodded again, this time scooping a kipper into her mouth.

He watched her, his gaze almost indulgent.

She set her plate aside and swallowed the bite she'd just taken. "Marcus..." She spoke his name softly, her voice barely above a whisper. "I'm so glad you're home."

"So am I. If only I'd known what was happening at the time, I would have–"

"You were fighting on the Continent," she said, interrupting him before he'd gotten out the words. "What could you have done while so far away? You wouldn't have abandoned your post to come to Hugh's aid. If you had, they would have shot you as a deserter."

His eyes, the auburn-black of charred chestnuts, reflected his anger. "That's where you're wrong, Lara. I would have thought of something to get myself back here in time to help. I would *done* something. He's my best friend."

"For this very reason, Hugh kept the news from you. He did not want your life ruined for his sake."

He took a sip of his coffee then calmly set down his cup. "Lara, I want your promise on an important matter."

"Promises are meant to be broken," she muttered, still feeling the hurt of her broken betrothal.

"No, they're not. I will not allow you to break this one."

She was at the end of her tether and he was piling demands on her? "If you want me to promise that I'll stay home and behave like a lady, knitting scarves and embroidering handkerchiefs while the lives of my father and brother continue to be destroyed, I'll tell you right now I will not agree to it. They are not going to hang Hugh while there's breath left in me."

"Lara—"

"They've dragged my father's reputation through the muck, imprisoned him in his own home, and may soon start confiscating his holdings. I will not sit idly by and do nothing. I am not a useless lump of clay. I would have clawed my way into Portsmouth Prison to free my brother, if I'd had to."

"But you didn't."

She frowned at him. "Only because he managed to escape on his own. But I was on my way there and ready to do it. No one, not even my father, was going to stop me. Nor will I be stopped now. Not here or anywhere. I will shoot any trespasser who dares take so much as a grain of corn from our Stratton estates. Lord Wexley, that cowardly, pathetic excuse for a weasel who broke off our betrothal a month before our wedding was to take place, asked the same of me and I refused."

Marcus was usually very hard to read, but she detected his lips twitch in amusement. She deepened her frown, for there was nothing laughable about a broken betrothal and she hadn't expected Marcus to be so callous.

"I'm sure the decision to distance himself from you and your family was not an easy one for him to make," he said, keeping his steady gaze on her as he spoke. "In truth, he must have loved you very much to hold out hope for as long as he did."

"He didn't love me." She tried to keep the heartache out of her voice, but the words came out in a breathy tremble and Marcus noticed. "He was enamored of my dowry. As soon as he realized it was about to be confiscated, the slimy toad couldn't run away from me fast enough. He knew the charges against my father and Hugh were all lies, a villainous put up job, but he didn't care. Nor did he or his family ever lift a finger to help me. To my shame, I even stooped to begging him. He refused."

"Not well done of Wexley. You're better off rid of him. Did you love him, Lara?"

She could not bear to meet his gaze, for he would clearly see into her very soul. "I thought I did. He was a cheerful fellow and nice looking. It was my first Season out and I was swept up in the excitement of it all, the glamor and pageantry. When this handsome man began to court me, I convinced myself I could love him. I had it all planned out to marry this nice man and live happily as friends throughout our marriage."

She began to toy with her table linen, twisting it in her hands as she spoke. "It feels like a dream now. The balls and musicales. The laughter and gaiety. The young ladies all looked so beautiful in their sparkling jewels, and silks and satins. The gentlemen all looked so handsome in black tie and tails. Everyone spoke of advantageous alliances. This marriage mart business leeches into one's brain, doesn't it? Especially when one is young and impressionable. I was too young to be out in Society. I understand that now."

She paused to glance at Marcus. "I didn't want to have a come-out. Who would want me with my family in disgrace? My father insisted upon it. He hoped someone would take me, that I'd be married off quickly and kept out of the family troubles. A dear friend of my mother's, Matilda, Duchess of Hartford, took me under her wing and sponsored me since my father could not."

She gave Marcus no chance to comment before she continued, her voice now filled with resolve. "We've gone off the point. No, I will not promise to sit by and do nothing while my father and brother meet their doom."

He regarded her calmly. "That isn't the promise I sought."

She blushed, realizing she'd gone on and on like a fool while he'd waited patiently to get a word in edgewise. "Oh, what then?"

"If things get tough and it looks as though they will..." He shifted his big body closer and caught her chin between his thumb and forefinger to keep her from turning away. *Oh, heavens!* The fierceness of this man could make the devil himself tremble. "I want you to promise me..."

"I've just told you. I hate promises." She pursed her lips in exasperation. "Can we not proceed without them?"

His gaze did not falter. "No, Lara. We cannot."

She was unraveling again. She needed Marcus in more ways than she cared to admit. She was angry he sought to negotiate terms. How could he do this while her heart was breaking? Yet, even while angry with him, she wanted to fall into his arms and kiss him.

She was angry that her body responded to him in ways she did not understand, nor did she wish to understand her feelings for him right now. "Fine, I'll give you all the promises you want." Slipping out of his grasp, she rose and took a step closer to his chair, her hands curled into fists. "I promise I will burn down that odious creature Dunning's courthouse if I must."

He eased back in his chair. "Still not the promise I seek."

"Here's another one for you then. I promise I will take down Portsmouth Prison stone by stone if they lock up my brother there again."

"Are you done?"

"No, I'm not done. I'm not nearly through raging." Her chin wobbled. She was going to cry again. "Drat it, Marcus. Just say what it is you want from me."

Since she was standing, he must have considered it impolite to remain seated, so he rose as well. Only he was a full head taller than she was and seemingly built of solid rock. "Lara…"

Oh, she could *feel* the roll of his tongue as he licked that "r".

"I want your promise that if we cannot save your father and brother—"

"We will. We must." The dastardly chin wobble resumed. *Not going to cry. Never going to cry again.*

"I understand. We will do everything we can. But if we cannot save them, then you must save yourself."

She looked at him, stunned. "You expect me to abandon them?"

"No, but you need to protect yourself. Your father

was right in wanting this when he thrust you out into Society. This is why," he said, taking her gently in his arms, "I must have your promise–"

"Do you not listen? I don't give promises."

"– to marry me."

Like what you read? Visit www. laurensmithbooks.com where you can sign up for my newsletter and never miss a new release. Follow me on Book Bub, Amazon, and join my VIP Reader Group on Facebook!

The Gentleman's Seduction

Standalone Stories

Tempted by A Rogue

Bewitching the Earl

Seducing an Heiress on a Train

Devil at the Gates

Sins and Scandals

An Earl By Any Other Name

A Gentleman Never Surrenders

A Scottish Lord for Christmas

Contemporary

The Surrender Series

The Gilded Cuff

The Gilded Cage

The Gilded Chain

The Darkest Hour

Love in London

Forbidden

Seduction

Climax

Forever Be Mine

Paranormal

Dark Seductions Series

The Shadows of Stormclyffe Hall

The Love Bites Series

The Bite of Winter

Brotherhood of the Blood Moon Series

Blood Moon on the Rise (coming soon)
Brothers of Ash and Fire
Grigori: A Royal Dragon Romance
Mikhail: A Royal Dragon Romance
Rurik: A Royal Dragon Romance

Sci-Fi Romance
Cyborg Genesis Series
Across the Stars
The Krinar Chronicles
The Krinar Eclipse

Buy these books today by visiting www.
laurensmithbooks.com
Or by visiting your favorite ebook/paperback book
store!

Lauren Smith is an Oklahoma attorney by day, author by night who pens adventurous and edgy romance stories by the light of her smart phone flashlight app. She knew she was destined to be a romance writer when she attempted to re-write the entire *Titanic* movie just to save Jack from drowning. Connecting with readers by writing emotionally moving, realistic and sexy romances no matter what time period is her passion. She's won multiple awards in several romance subgenres including: New England Reader's Choice Awards, Greater Detroit BookSeller's

Best Awards, and a Semi-Finalist award for the Mary Wollstonecraft Shelley Award.

To Connect with Lauren, visit her at:
www.laurensmithbooks.com
lauren@laurensmithbooks.com

 facebook.com/LaurenDianaSmith

twitter.com/LSmithAuthor

instagram.com/Laurensmithbooks

CPSIA information can be obtained
at www.ICGtesting.com
Printed in the USA
LVHW090105050921
696974LV00005B/589